D0956115

MARVEL

THE INCREDIBLE HULK

MARVEL

THE INCREDIBLE HULK

Adapted by ALEX IRVINE

Based on the Screen Story and Screenplay by ZAK PENN

Produced by AVI ARAD GALE ANNE HURD KEVIN FEIGE

Directed by LOUIS LETERRIER

LITTLE, BROWN AND COMPANY
New York Boston

marvelkids.com

© 2015 MARVEL

Little, Brown and Company

Hachette Book Group
1290 Avenue of the Americas, New York, NY 10104
Visit us at lb-kids.com

Little, Brown and Company is a division of Hachette Book Group, Inc.
The Little, Brown name and logo are trademarks of Hachette Book Group, Inc.

The publisher is not responsible for websites (or their content)
that are not owned by the publisher.

First Edition: January 2015

Library of Congress Cataloging-in-Publication Data

Irvine, Alexander (Alexander C.)
Phase one : the Incredible Hulk / adapted by Alex Irvine ; based on the screenplay by Zak Penn.—First edition.
pages cm.—(Marvel cinematic universe)
ISBN 978-0-316-25633-9 (hardcover)—ISBN 978-0-316-38354-7 (ebook)—ISBN 978-0-316-38355-4 (library edition ebook) 1. Graphic novels. I. Incredible Hulk (Motion picture) II. Title.
PZ7.7.I78Phm 2015
741.5'973—dc23

2014037461

10 9 8 7 6 5 4 3 2 1

RRD-C

Printed in the United States of America

PROLOGUE

He remembered the green light of the scanner playing across his face. He remembered the feeling of the gamma radiation, like a tingling heat on his skin. He remembered being scared when he felt his body start to change.

After that, things were confused. There was a chair smashing through a window. Wrecked lab equipment scattered across the room. Betty slumped on the floor. Crushed lab furniture and computers jumbled on top of

1

the two people beside her. General Ross, his uniform torn, scrambling.

A hole broken through a wall. Cool air. Screaming and sirens.

And anger, so much anger.

Then nothing.

The hospital room was blinding white. Betty was hooked up to tubes and life-support machines, unconscious. She looked so small.

A strong hand landed on his shoulder. He looked up to see General Ross staring at him. You've got a lot of nerve coming in here after what you did, *General Ross said.*

Bruce had never felt so tired in his life, so filled with misery. Worst of all was the rage that lingered in his blood. He could feel it, waiting for its chance to escape again. The monster wanted out, and he didn't know how long he could hold it back.

I just wanted to see her, *he said.* Make sure she's all right.

She'll be all right as soon as you leave her alone, *General Ross said*. Permanently. Steer clear of her. You're a project asset now. That's all.

He felt his pulse start to race, and knew the monster was waking up again. Terrified, he pushed past General Ross and ran—out of the hospital, out of the country, out of Betty's life. He didn't stop running.

CHAPTER 1

Bruce Banner sat straight up out of the nightmare, sweaty, his pulse racing. He reached over to the metronome he kept by his bed and put one hand on it, listening to its steady tick, tick, tick at sixty beats per minute. He tried to slow his pulse down to that rhythm. When he had gotten it under control, he stopped the device.

He woke up like that nearly every day, keeping the metronome going all night to give his unconscious mind a rhythm. So far he'd been able to keep himself from getting out of control for five months. That's how long it had been since the monster had gotten out.

He'd been in Rocinha Favela, Brazil, for about that long, hiding out in the jumble of shacks and apartment buildings. It was where the poor people lived, and the people who wanted to disappear. Bruce was both.

He made breakfast, then watched some TV with a Portuguese-English dictionary by his side. He was trying to learn the language and making decent progress. His dog, who he called Cachorro because it was the word for "dog," sat at his side begging.

Bruce looked up a word. He asked Cachorro if he was hungry in Portuguese. Cachorro's ears pricked up. Bruce gave him his plate to lick.

After washing up, he headed for his daily aikido practice. He'd never been a fighter, but aikido was good for teaching self-discipline, and since the... event...back at Culver University, Bruce knew he needed all the self-discipline he could get.

In the aikido gym, his instructor ran him through exercises and drills, ending up with a series of falls that had Bruce breathing hard. He knew his pulse was up over one hundred beats per minute. That wasn't dangerous territory, but it was a little too fast.

His instructor waved at him to sit. Then he sat opposite Bruce, both of them cross-legged. "Let's work on your breathing," he said in Portuguese.

Bruce nodded.

"Here...emotions," his instructor said, placing a palm flat on his chest. He touched his belly and huffed out short breaths. His belly pushed in with each one.

Bruce started doing it, too. Together they practiced breathing from the belly, using the diaphragm. "When you control your emotions, you control your body," his instructor said. "Now we'll control your pulse."

He slapped Bruce in the face, hard. Bruce held himself back from responding, but he felt his pulse quicken. Slap! His face stung and he felt the rage building. Bruce glanced down at his watch. His pulse was 146.

Too high.

He breathed. He did exactly what his instructor had showed, letting the breath flow deep into his belly and come back out. Slowly his pulse came back down to a more normal rate.

"You're learning," his instructor said.

It was time to go to work at the bottling plant, making sure thousands of bottles of guarana soda got where they were supposed to go every day. The beans at the Brazilian guarana plant had three times as much caffeine as coffee. It definitely wasn't something Bruce was going to drink. Not when it was so important to keep his pulse down. He didn't even drink tea or eat chocolate anymore because they contained caffeine.

He filed into the plant along with the other day laborers, finding a place in the dingy, poorly lit locker room between the main gate and the factory floor. As Bruce put his bag in his locker, someone banged into him hard from behind. He looked up and saw one of the factory's tough guys cruising on down the hall.

Most of his coworkers were just regular people, but there were a few bullies in every crowd.

If only the bully knew what Bruce could do to him...

No.

He shrugged it off and went to work.

His job was basically to do a bunch of different jobs. He distributed the mail, loaded pallets of soda for shipping, and kept track of where everything was going. Today they were putting together a shipment headed to the United States, specifically the Milwaukee and Chicago areas. .

First on the agenda today was distributing the mail. Bruce brought things to a couple dozen people throughout the bottling plant, including a young woman named Martina, who was friendly to him and occasionally helped him with the language. She also lived two floors below him at the favela.

The snap of an electrical short came from the catwalk up above the conveyor belts that snaked all over the factory floor, carrying bottles to be filled and capped. The upper level was where the managers watched and kept track of everything. They also stopped and started the different lines to make sure everything stayed coordinated.

"Breakdown! Breakdown!" the owner called from up on the catwalk. He beckoned for Bruce, who had fixed many of the factory's outdated machines already during his time there. Bruce went up to the catwalk and saw that the control switch operating the main filling conveyor belt had shorted out. He put his glasses on to look at the wiring. After stripping the wires so they had better contact and winding them around the button anchors again, he tried it out.

The conveyor belt kicked into motion. "Okay," Bruce said. "I can make it work for a while, but you need new..." He trailed off, not knowing the Portuguese word for "resistors."

"I need a new factory," the owner said. "Five months you've been helping me out like this. You're too smart for day labor. Let me put you on the payroll."

Bruce smiled and shrugged as he put the cover back on the control switch. He glanced over at the manager again—and that's when he cut his thumb on a sharp edge.

It wasn't a terrible cut, but it bled quickly. Droplets fell through the catwalk onto the moving conveyor belt below.

"No, no, no, shut that off!" Bruce shouted. "Turn it off!" He was already running, trying to track the exact spot where the blood had fallen. "Watch out!" he said as he pushed past one of his surprised coworkers.

The manager stopped the conveyor belt, and Bruce ran along the line until he found the spot where the blood drops had fallen. He carefully wiped them up with a rag from his pocket, scrubbing hard until all the blood was gone. Then he closed the cut with a little tube of Super Glue he kept in the same pocket with the rag. It was his emergency-cut kit and he was never without it because Bruce knew how dangerous his blood could be.

"Okay," he sighed. The line started up again.

That had been close, Bruce thought. He hoped he'd gotten all the blood.

He then wrapped up the pallet of just-filled bottles for shipping. He put the address label on the shrink-wrap and headed off for lunch.

On his way, he saw the guy who had bumped into him in the locker room. Now he was giving Martina a hard time, cornering her and touching her face, telling her how pretty she was. His friends watched and made rude comments.

Bruce hesitated. He didn't want to cause trouble, but he couldn't just stand there and let Martina get harassed. He took a few steps toward her.

"Martina," he called out in Portuguese. "Want to come have lunch with me?"

"Get lost, gringo," the leader snapped at Bruce.

Bruce kept his eyes on Martina. "How about it?"

The group leader stuck his arm out in front of Bruce. "I said beat it," he growled. "You want a problem?"

Bruce raised his hands. "No problem," he said.

"Too late," the guy said. He shoved Bruce in the chest. His friends muscled in closer to Bruce on all sides.

Bruce's pulse began to race. He glanced down at

the pulse monitor on his wrist—it was climbing fast, past 100 beats per minute, heading for 120. "Okay, listen," he told them in his broken Portuguese. "Don't make me hungry. You wouldn't like me when I'm—" Bruce bit his lip, realizing he'd mixed up a word. "No, wait...that's not right..."

The leader looked puzzled for a moment. Then, thinking Bruce was mocking him, he shoved Bruce again, causing another spike in Bruce's pulse. Things might have really gone wrong, but the manager saw the ruckus and shouted down from the catwalk.

"Get moving! Get out of here!"

The bully and his friends pushed past, laughing like it was no big deal, but from the looks on their faces, Bruce knew he'd be a fool to be caught alone with them.

As soon as they were gone, Martina let out a big sigh and thanked Bruce. He smiled at her, carefully controlling his breathing, and then went on to eat his lunch.

CHAPTER 2

When the final whistle of the day sounded, Bruce headed outside and was excited to see the supply driver waiting for him. He was one of the guys who moonlighted doing unofficial delivery runs between the jungle and the city. A week or so before, Bruce had asked him to find a specific flower. He had it! Bruce ran over and paid him. Then he hurried home with the rare orchids, feeling a surge of optimism to balance out the stressful day.

When Bruce got home, he showed the package to Cachorro. "See that?" he said excitedly. "That's our ticket out of here."

Cachorro barked, picking up on Bruce's excitement. Bruce put the flowers down and set up his laptop and portable satellite uplink. He kept them hidden in the apartment, together with a newspaper clipping.

On the paper was a grainy, printed-out photograph of a beautiful woman with refined features and long dark hair. The caption read *Dr. Elizabeth Ross*. Bruce sighed. Betty Ross had been his girlfriend as well as his lab partner in the experiment that had gone so wrong. He missed her desperately, but he would never let himself be in a position to hurt her again. She didn't know where he was now, and he was going to stay hidden until he solved his problem.

It had been a long time since he'd seen Betty. She might not love him anymore after what had happened at Culver, but the thought of her was the only thing that kept Bruce going sometimes. He fired up the satellite feed and used an encrypted chat program to contact a person he knew only as Mr. Blue. Bruce had spent the past months trying to reach out to people who knew something about gamma radiation. Mr. Blue clearly did, and Bruce relied on his scientific advice. He was a skilled research scientist himself, but he had no lab and no way to keep up on the latest findings in his area—at least not if he wanted to stay hidden and stay safe.

> G: Blue, are you there?
> B: Mr. Green? Good hearing from you, my
>   mysterious friend.
> G: I've found it.
> B: At long last! It's a lovely little flower, isn't it?

Bruce looked at the flower. It was pretty, but that's not why he cared about it. He returned to the monitor and his encrypted conversation. Mr. Blue had already logged off after leaving a final note:

> B: Be sure to try a high dose. Good luck! :)

Bruce signed off and got to work. First he clipped the orchid's petals into small pieces. He gathered them in a small bowl and poured a bit of rubbing alcohol in before crushing the flower into a paste. He added more fluid and put the mixture into a makeshift centrifuge he'd built using parts from a bicycle. It spun most of the fluid out into a small vial, where Bruce examined it. It was still too cloudy, meaning there were still too many bits of the crushed petals. He needed a better filter. He lit his stove and slowly heated the mixture in a distilling setup, watching the purer fluid fall drop by drop into a new vial. Now it was clear. Now he could use it.

After pricking his finger, Bruce squeezed a drop of his blood onto a glass slide. He peered down at the slide through a microscope and adjusted the focus until he could see individual little disk-shaped red blood cells. Only his weren't smooth and red; they were lumpy and a mixture of red and green, like they had been since his accident. This was the effect of the gamma radiation he'd been exposed to during the experiment. It was also what caused his transformation into...that thing.

Bruce took out the slide. He filled an eyedropper

with the clear fluid he'd distilled from the crushed orchid petals. Then he squeezed out three drops onto his blood on the slide and stuck the slide back under the microscope.

Peering into the eyepiece, Bruce saw the formula seeping into his blood from the edges. The green lumps disappeared, and what were left were ordinary cells. Bruce's heart jumped. Could he have found a cure? Could he finally come out of hiding and go home?

Could he see Betty again?

But as he kept watching, scribbling in a lab notebook to record the experiment...his cells deformed again, with the warty green bumps coming back and spreading to how they had been before.

The experiment was a failure, and Bruce felt sick with the loss of hope. Eventually, Bruce got up from the lab table and went to his laptop to tell Mr. Blue the disappointing results.

G: Another failure.
B: How much did you use?
G: All of it.

B: Then it's time to meet.

G: Not safe.

B: Living with gamma poisoning is not safe. Stop messing with flowers. Send me a sample.

B: Can't help if you won't let me.

Bruce looked at the picture of Betty and at the litter of flower stems on his table. Mr. Blue was right. He'd done everything he could do without actually giving someone else a look at a sample of his blood.

When you only had one option, there was no point wasting time. Bruce drew a few milliliters of his blood with a syringe, capped the tube, and wrapped it carefully for shipping. He labeled it *Mr. Green*. The next day he mailed a package to Mr. Blue's post office box in New York City.

CHAPTER 3

In his Pentagon office, General Thaddeus Ross—known to friends and enemies alike as Thunderbolt—snapped out of his reverie when his assistant, Major Kathleen Sparr, put a stack of forms onto his desk. Ross signed the forms automatically. They were basic requisition orders, dull and routine.

"Here's something a bit more interesting," Sparr said. She held out a fax. "Possible gamma sickness.

Milwaukee. A man drank one of those guarana sodas. Guess it had a little more kick than he was looking for."

"Where was the soda bottled?" Ross asked.

Major Sparr checked the fax. "Racinho Favela, Brazil."

A few weeks before, intelligence had flagged something else in Racinho Favela. A smuggler had been asking around about a particular rare orchid. It was known to S.H.I.E.L.D. scientists to have anti-radiation sickness possibilities. Ross and Sparr had tried to find out who had ordered the flower and where, but the Brazilian wilderness was a hard place to get good intelligence and the lead had petered out.

Now, though, a bottle of soda from the same city had turned up tainted with gamma radiation. That couldn't possibly be a coincidence.

"Get our agency people looking for an American at that bottling plant," Ross ordered. "Tell them no contact. If he even sees them, he's gone."

Then he got on the phone to call in some favors from an old friend.

Two hours later, a transport van stopped near the runway of Fort Johnson, deep in the Florida Everglades. Ross watched with his fellow general, Joe Greller. "I got you what I could," Greller said. "Short notice, but they're all quality. And I pulled you an ace."

The chatter stopped as a helicopter banked in for a landing. Before the chopper was fully at rest, a short, muscular soldier with dirty blond hair leaped out. There was nothing remarkable about his features except his eyes. They were the eyes of a man who saw everything just a little bit better than most.

"Emil Blonsky," Greller said. "Born in Russia, raised in England. On loan to SOCOM from the Royal Marines." SOCOM was the United States Special Operations Command.

"I know you cashed in some chips for this, Joe," Ross said.

Greller shrugged. "Glad I could help. Just make it good."

As the plane buzzed toward Brazil, Major Sparr handed out briefing folders containing photos of Bruce Banner, Bruce's apartment building, and the town of Racinho Favela. The commandos studied them.

"This is the target and the location," Sparr lectured. "Snatch and grab only. Live capture. You'll have dart clips and suppression ordinance, but live fire is for backup only. We've got local help, but we want it tight and quiet."

Ross joined the briefing in the rear of the plane. Blonsky looked up at him. "Is he a fighter?" Blonsky asked.

"Your target is a fugitive from the US government who stole military secrets," Ross replied curtly. "He is also implicated in the deaths of two scientists, a military officer, an Idaho state trooper, and possibly two Canadian hunters. So don't wait to see if he's a fighter. Tranq him and bring him back."

Blonsky nodded.

CHAPTER 4

That night Bruce was relaxing, trying to stay cool, when a chime sounded from his laptop. Mr. Blue was contacting him over the encrypted channel. Bruce hopped out of bed and hurried to the table.

B: Good news. Preliminary blood tests show significant gamma reduction.

Hardly daring to believe it, Bruce typed:

> G: Will it cure me?
> B: Yes.
> B: But...I need more data.

"Oh, come on," Bruce said. Mr. Blue was still typing.

> B: Exposure levels, gamma concentration, cell
> saturation...
> G: Impossible. Data is not here.
> B: Where is it?
> G: HOME.

Frustrated, Bruce closed the laptop and sat for a long while, looking at the picture of Betty. Again, just when it looked like he might be making some progress, he was cut off. He'd almost allowed himself to hope that he'd be able to find the cure himself, and then he'd be able to go home. Maybe he and Betty could have picked up where they'd left off before the accident....

But no. Now it didn't look like that would be possible at all.

CHAPTER 5

As Bruce slept, Cachorro stretched against his feet. The night sounds of the city—car horns, a distant siren, a radio playing a samba-reggae mix—echoed softly in the apartment. Somewhere down the hill, a dog barked. It was an ordinary evening in Racinho Favela...except for the commando operation just now swinging into action.

At the base of one of they alleys that wound up the steep hillside, a commando scanned the area with night-vision goggles. Between two tenement buildings he saw a narrow walkway that rose at a sharp angle toward the target location. Laundry flapped on clothes-lines. The commando signaled to the other soldiers.

Five figures stepped out of the shadows, and the squad moved up the alley in formation, their black uniforms making them seem like shadows themselves. They carried dart rifles and had backup MP5 submachine guns slung over their shoulders. The few people still out at this hour saw them and steered clear, not wanting any trouble. Ahead of them, at the top of a short flight of stairs, a dog stood barking.

In Bruce's apartment, the sound of the dog barking stopped. Cachorro looked up and growled.

The commandos climbed the stairs and continued up the alley, stepping over the tranquilized dog. Guided by handheld Geiger counters, they zeroed in on the target, a four-story tenement built into the hillside near the top of the ridge.

At the base of the hill, General Ross, Major Sparr, and a Brazilian officer supervised the commandos' progress from the command vehicle, which was filled with surveillance equipment. Ross monitored the gamma-radiation levels on the feeds from the Geiger counters. They ticked up sharply as the commando team approached the target structure. "Gentlemen," he said, "here we go."

When the soldiers reached Bruce's apartment building, Blonsky hand-signaled for one of them to head for the roof, using an interior stairwell since the building had no fire escape. Blonsky then motioned for two of the commandos to approach the target's door. Geiger counters ticked softly. One soldier dropped into a crouch and snaked a miniature video camera attached to a thin flexible rod under the door.

The soldier couldn't see any movement on the tiny monitor. He adjusted his device and was startled by the sight of a giant dog's muzzle sniffing the camera. A tongue blotted out his view as the dog licked the lens. Then it backed away and he could see again. The target appeared to be asleep in his bed.

The soldier with the camera held up one finger and then pointed it to the right, signaling that one person inside was low to the ground. Another soldier applied small blobs of plastic explosive to the hinges and lock. Blonsky stepped back and faced the door, his tranquilizer gun ready.

He keyed a code into his microphone communicator.

When Sparr received Blonsky's signal, she turned her attention to the monitors, which showed feeds from one of the team's helmet cameras, one from the back of the building, and one from the soldier on the roof.

Everything was in place. Ross nodded. "Take him," he ordered Blonsky.

Boom! The explosives ignited, blowing the door off its hinges.

Before the door had hit the floor, Blonsky hustled into Bruce's apartment, with the other commandos right behind him sweeping the apartment for hostiles. The target's dog barked furiously as Blonsky cleared the doorway, stepped to his right, and and fired three tranq darts at the sleeping form. Each dart hit its target—one dart in the torso, and one in each of his legs.

The target didn't move. That was unusual; the tranquilizer worked fast, but it wasn't instantaneous.

Suspicious, Blonsky slowly approached the bed. He yanked the covers back.

On the pillow was a Styrofoam head covered with a wig and a baseball cap. Blonsky ripped the covers all the way off, revealing bunched-up pillows on the bed. The target's dog was still barking and Blonsky, irritated, silenced it with a tranq dart.

Then he saw the rope dangling out the window over the kitchen sink. Blonsky activated his microphone. "Target's on the move," he reported.

CHAPTER 6

With his backpack over his shoulders, Bruce lowered himself from his kitchen window, down the outside of the building. His time in the gym had paid off. Before...the event...he wouldn't have had the strength to do this.

As he descended, the door right below him opened and Martina looked out, drawn by the commotion upstairs. She gasped when she saw Bruce. He shushed her and she let him in, shutting the door behind him.

Bruce heard Cachorro stop barking up in his apartment. He hoped the commandos hadn't hurt him. He also heard what they were saying to each other. "Target's on the move," one of them had reported, and then a moment later, "He's on the ground."

Footsteps thumped above as the commandos searched Bruce's apartment and headed out in pursuit, assuming Bruce was on the run. He waited in Martina's apartment, crouching by the door, until they were gone into the mazelike alleys of the favela. Below, on the street, he heard someone gunning a powerful engine. Probably a military support vehicle. This had to be an American operation, even though at least one of the voices coming from upstairs had sounded British.

When it had been quiet for a minute, Bruce nodded at Martina, and she nervously opened her front door and glanced outside. She shook her head: nothing out there.

With no time even to thank her, Bruce fled the apartment and hustled at a controlled walk down the street with the hood of his sweatshirt over his head. He took an indirect route down to the street, using the confusing alleys to his advantage. Along the way he caught a glimpse of the black van and the black-clad commando guarding it. Unfortunately the commando saw him, too. Bruce froze, just for a moment—but the suspicious reaction was all the commando needed. He started calling to the rest of his team.

Bruce broke into a sprint, turning down the street. His heart rate was rising, inching up past eighty beats per minute. He had to stay calm. Otherwise the monster would get out and everyone could be in danger.

Behind him, the commandos were in hot pursuit. Bruce doubled back away from the main street again and worked his way downhill, ducking under hanging laundry, leaping over baskets, careening across courtyards. Blonsky and his partner followed close behind, anticipating Bruce's turns through the labyrinth of alleys.

When Bruce reached a paved street with fewer people, he bolted at full speed. He had to stop short when his path ended at a steep hillside with a sheer drop to the houses below. Bruce jumped onto the nearest roof and, jumping from one to the next, ran across the tops of the squat buildings. His feet pounded on the rusty tin, and shouts of complaint bellowed up from the occupants inside.

Blonsky and his partner reached the hillside a few seconds later, in time to see Bruce jumping from house to house. Blonsky scanned the area, looking for a faster way down. Two other commandos had a different line of pursuit. They were right on the target's tail.

Meanwhile, the black van circled around the slum at top speed to catch Bruce if he came out the other side. Ross and Sparr stayed glued to their video monitors, watching the chaotic green-lit images of the chase.

Bruce reached an area thick with laundry, and the flapping sheets almost obscured the edge of a roof. He whipped through the cloth, his hood slipping back as he jumped down to another level of roofs.

The two commandos following him hit the same patch of clotheslines, but the taller soldier missed the blind jump. He fell hard, rolled to a standing position, and headed downhill, knowing the target had to come out on the main street sooner or later.

Bruce reached the end of the residential area and

hopped down from the last roof into a party area of bars and late-night clubs. The streets here were crowded with people out for a good time; it would be easier to disappear. But he had to stop. His pulse was hammering, up toward 170, and that was monster territory. Pressing himself into a rack of empty bottles at the back of a restaurant, Bruce worked himself through a quick set of mental exercises. He knew he didn't have much time. As soon as he got it down toward 150, he looked out—only to see one of the commandos.

The commando raised his gun and fired. Bruce heard the dart go by, too slow to be a bullet. They were trying to tranquilize him. He launched himself into the midst of the crowd, turned right, getting a step on the pursuing commandos again.

Blonsky charged after Bruce but the crowds on the narrow sidewalk slowed him down. The operation was no longer quiet, but it could still be successful. He lost visual contact and shoved through the crowds, looking for a sign of where the target might have gone.

Bruce checked his pulse monitor: 160...165...He was in trouble. His pulse was too high, and he was really sweating now. He veered into an alley, rushed around a corner, and popped out onto a side street, almost running into the black van's open door.

Seated inside was General Thunderbolt Ross.

Ross looked up and, for a dizzying second, he locked eyes with Bruce. It was the first time they'd seen each other in five years.

Bruce broke into motion just as fast as he stopped, and launched into another alley. Ross. He should have known.

Bruce reeled through the narrow street, breathing hard. When the alley ended, he took a hard right down a busy, wide street filled with restaurants. Bruce glanced back to see if anyone was following him, and he slammed right into a group of four men. Bruce recognized them as the tough guys from the bottling plant, led by the one who'd been harassing Martina—and he could tell from the looks on their faces that they recognized him, too. His stomach sank.

The guys were rowdy and looking for a fight. And for them, no one better than Bruce could have shown up at that exact moment. The problem was, Bruce couldn't afford to fight. He couldn't spare the time, or Ross's commandos would catch him, and he couldn't take the stress...or the monster would get out.

The leader of the group stepped up and threw a wild punch at Bruce, who saw it coming a mile away. His aikido training kicked in; he caught the guy's sleeve and used his own momentum to send him crashing into a pile of trash.

Before the man's friends could react, Bruce ran, skidding into another side alley. Behind him, he could hear pursuit. Now he had commandos and local dirtbags chasing him. Great.

At the end of the alleyway, Bruce found himself outside the bottling factory. With little time to think, he raced toward it.

At the same time, the commandos had narrowed their pursuit. They knew the target couldn't be far. General Ross had just seen him, and from the van's location, there was only one way the target could have gone without one of the team spotting him. Blonsky climbed back onto a low-hanging roof and surveyed the town. He spotted a group of locals slipping through the loosely chained back gate of a small factory. They were chasing someone, and Blonsky had a feeling he knew who.

"Where is he?" General Ross demanded over the comlink.

"Target acquired," Blonsky reported.

CHAPTER 7

In the factory changing room, Bruce heaved deep breaths, his back against the wall. He listened to the drip of the showers as he tried to lower his pulse rate, slowly easing it down from a very dangerous 187 toward a safer 100 beats per minute.

A noise on the factory floor startled him, and his pulse jumped again. It was the tough guys.

He couldn't stay in the locker room, waiting to be found. He crept out amid the machinery, pausing every few seconds to listen for footsteps. He could hear the men whispering, drunkenly following him. Their leader would want Bruce's head on a stick for interfering with his pursuit of Martina—and for the embarrassment of having the manager yell at them like schoolchildren. If a fight became inevitable, so would ...

No. No monster today.

Bruce threaded through the banks of bottling machines, getting closer to the far side of the factory, where he could see an exit sign dimly glowing green. Under it was a steel door. He pushed gently on the latch and escaped.

The leader was waiting for him. He laughed and shoved Bruce back into the factory. Bruce stumbled backward and then turned to run, but the other tough guys were standing behind him. They gathered around Bruce and began to shove and kick him against the machines.

Bruce caught one of them with an elbow and got free for a moment, but the others pinned him against the wall.

"Please," Bruce begged, "don't do this." His pulse hit 140 beats per minute.

The leader pulled off Bruce's backpack and slapped his face. "What?" the leader sneered. He flung the backpack away.

"No! Not the computer!" Bruce said. He was still gasping for breath, and his pulse was starting to get out of his control.

"Not so tough now, huh? Try those fancy moves again. Come on, we all want to see." He gave Bruce a hard push, and Bruce fell back onto a knobby piece of equipment, crying out in agony.

The commandos raced into the factory and heard the confrontation. Blonsky signaled for his men to split up, and he slid on his night-vision goggles. He could see the heat signatures of a cluster of men, glowing neon green in the darkness.

The four guys continued to bully Bruce with two of them pinning him against a labeling machine.

"Please stop," cried Bruce. His pulse climbed to 150 beats per minute. "Me. Angry. Very bad," he said in Portuguese.

"You bad angry?" the leader replied. "I bad angry!"

Behind him, Bruce spotted a quick motion in the shadows. A black-clad figure crouched in the dim light. Panic flooded his body, and Bruce's pulse shot up to 175, climbing rapidly to 190...then higher...

"You don't understand!" he yelled. "Something really bad is going to happen here!"

"Yeah," the leader agreed, "something bad *is* going to happen."

A commando's night-vision scope alighted on Bruce's face, then dropped its sight on his neck.

Bruce saw a gleaming tranquilizer gun's muzzle, peeking out from the shadows. He lunged to the side, pulling the tough guys with him. The leader punched Bruce in the gut, and Bruce crumpled.

Blonsky fired the tranq gun, missing Bruce but nailing one of the other men in the neck.

Bruce gasped as his pulse leaped past two hundred, his heart throbbing.

Blonsky peered through his night-vision goggles at the cluster of green men. One of the shapes dropped where the tranq had hit him, and another was already huddled on the floor. *Maybe Banner is a fighter after all*, he thought. Then a strange blast of green light flared. All the commandos' Geiger counters spiked.

In the van, Ross saw the radiation spike and bolted forward in his chair.

Blonsky ripped off his night-vision goggles, then signaled for the other commandos to hold position. He watched as the tough guys, the two who were still upright, nervously backed away.

Blonsky couldn't clearly see what was happening, but it looked like Bruce was being twisted into strange shapes. Then Bruce let out an anguished scream, and a strange tearing sound filled the factory. "Anybody else seeing this?" asked one of the other commandos.

All of them were. Where Bruce had been lying on the ground, groaning in pain, now there was... something else.

"Shut up!" the leader hissed, and he launched a kick at Bruce's warping body. That was the worst mistake of his life. His foot met something insanely hard. Almost too fast to see, the leader was launched upward by his leg, across the expanse of the factory. He crashed through an office window and hit the wall hard enough to leave a dent in the sheet metal. The sounds were nearly drowned out by an inhuman howl from the creature in the shadows.

When the roar faded, everyone in the factory fell silent.

Then, yelling, the remaining bully bolted from the shadows. An enormous, muscular arm reached out after him. He was dragged screaming into the darkness, and a moment later, his body was flung back out into the open, sprawled on the factory floor.

"We've got a bogey of some kind," one of the commandos said. "Please advise."

"That is the target!" Ross roared. "Use every tranq you've got! Do it now!"

Two of the soldiers advanced toward where the giant lurked between enormous liquid tanks. They rapidly fired their tranquilizer darts into the darkness. The projectiles fell to the concrete floor, their needles bent as if they'd hit a wall.

A massive foot stepped out of the shadows and crushed the darts. The beast charged, heaving the bottling tanks out of the way with unbelievable strength. The creature then stomped toward the commandos.

Soldiers whipped out their submachine guns. "Go live!" one screeched. Bottles exploded around the factory, and the bullets ricocheted off the roof. The commandos pulled together into a tight formation, moving through the factory and searching for their target.

Blonsky and his partner ducked behind a bank of machinery. The body of one commando landed nearby, hitting an ON switch. The machinery roared to life, trundling broken bottles down the belt with loud clanks and bright blinking lights.

Between another set of vast tanks, Blonsky saw that the creature was on the move. His partner opened fire, but the tanks prevented a clear shot.

Blonsky spotted a set of stairs to the catwalks above. He raced for it while his partner backed up two other commandos firing at the creature. They could see they were hitting it, but the bullets were bouncing off, ricocheting into machinery and pinging to the ground. The creature didn't even slow down.

Up on the catwalk, Blonsky peered down as the creature disappeared into a cloud of steam in an open middle area. His partner pulled an antipersonnel grenade off his belt and hurled it into the steam. The soldiers ducked for cover.

The grenade hit something and detonated, rocking the factory. The beast's massive form was outlined by the explosion, but then steam covered him again.

The soliders waited. No way anyone was walking away from that, Blonsky thought.

Then the pounding of heavy feet shook the floor. A roar and sickening sound of tearing steel echoed through the room. Out of the steam, a gargantuan metal tank lurched forward, like a gigantic sled, pushed by the giant. It clipped the supports of the catwalk under Blonsky and smashed into the soldiers on the ground. The commandos screamed as they got caught in the heaving machinery. It smashed into the far wall of the factory, rupturing in a fountain of green guarana soda.

In the van, the soldiers' cameras blinked off, the monitors turning black. All Sparr and Ross could hear over the microphones was moaning.

Inside the factory, Blonsky sprinted along the catwalk above the creature, looking for a clean shot. He got one when he reached the corner. His bullets raked across the beast's shoulder blades.

He was humanoid but the size of three men. Four, maybe. And green. His skin looked like it was stretched to the limit over unbelievable masses of muscle.

Enraged, the creature spun around, swatting the bullets out of the air with his giant hands.

Blonsky reloaded his weapon, his eyes remaining locked on his target. But then he froze in awe as the beast stepped out fully from the shadows.

The creature glared up at him with rage, then snarled and flexed his shoulders, grabbing a forklift and hurling it easily up at Blonsky like he was throwing a baseball.

Blonsky dove to the side as the machinery crashed into the catwalk where he'd just been standing. The catwalk lurched and Blonsky hung on desperately.

The creature grabbed a steel block of machinery off the assembly line and hurled it. This projectile wasn't aimed at Blonsky. With an earsplitting crash, it smashed a gaping hole through the wall of the factory.

"No!" General Ross shouted. He was not going to come this close and then miss Bruce. He pulled the van's door open and dashed outside.

"Sir, no!" Sparr shouted.

Ross had just reached the side of the bottling plant when the wall exploded in front of him. He ducked around a corner for cover, then peered around the edge.

The giant stepped out of the hole, his eyes glinting as he looked around. Then he took off running.

Ross watched, his chest heaving, as the beast barreled away into the night.

CHAPTER 8

After the factory, Ross's team searched Bruce's apartment. A forensics technician inspected Bruce's homemade lab while Sparr riffled through his belongings.

"The stuff in the bottles were basic lab chemicals," Sparr reported to Ross. "He was cooking something, but there's no trace of it. He zeroed the place. Not a scrap of paper. Like he knew we were coming."

"He didn't know," Ross replied. "He's just always ready to leave."

Then Blonsky entered the apartment, carrying Bruce's backpack. "I knew something was different before I shot the first tranq," he said. "He had it on him when he bolted."

"Tell me that's what I'm hoping it is," Sparr said. She took the backpack and emptied it, pulling out a laptop. A grainy printout of a picture fell out, and Blonsky picked it up.

"Is that a girlfriend?" Blonsky wondered, examining the photo of Betty Ross. "She helps him maybe?"

General Ross snatched the picture of his daughter out of Blonsky's hands. "*She* is no longer a factor," he said. "We closed that door to him long ago. He's alone. He wants to be alone." He tapped the laptop. "But see if he's been talking to anybody."

Blonsky stepped between Ross and Sparr. "Forgive me, sir," he said "But does somebody want to talk about what went down in there? Because he didn't lose us and he wasn't alone. We had him and something

51

hit us. Something *big*." Getting frustrated when Ross didn't respond, Blonsky raised his voice. "It threw a forklift!"

Calming himself, he added, "It was the most powerful thing I've ever seen."

"Well, it's gone," Ross said.

"If Banner knows what it is," Blonsky swore, "I'm going to track him down and I'm going to put my foot on his throat and—"

Ross cleared his throat. "That *was* Banner."

Blonsky shifted nervously. "You're going to have to explain that statement, sir."

"No, I don't," Ross replied. "You've done a good job. Pack up and get our men on the plane. We're going home." Then he strode out of Bruce's apartment.

Sparr and Blonsky started after the general, dumbstruck.

Bruce woke to birdsong in the forest. He'd fallen asleep on a rock at the base of a waterfall....Well, "sleep"

wasn't really the right word. Somehow the creature had run out of rage, or energy, here. Then it had just stopped, and Bruce had become himself again. He looked at his hands, his pale and ordinary hands. His only clothing was a shredded pair of pants. He had to hold them up as he walked. Groaning, he followed a muddy road out of the woods until he reached a paved highway cutting through the mountains.

Bruce waved down a truck and leaned in the passenger-side window. "Can you help me?" he asked the driver in Portuguese.

"No habla portugués," the driver replied.

Spanish? People in Brazil didn't speak Spanish. Which meant, Bruce realized, that he was no longer in Brazil. But... *"¿Dónde estoy?"* Bruce asked. Where am I?

"Guatemala," the driver said.

Guatemala? That was all the way north across Central America from Brazil. Somehow Bruce had traveled more than three thousand miles while he was ... while the monster had been loose.

"I'm going to the next town," the driver added in

5 3

Spanish. He didn't ask what Bruce was doing in the middle of the rain forest dressed only in a pair of pants that barely stayed up.

"Will you help me?" Bruce asked.

The driver leaned across and opened the door. "Get in."

When Bruce was in the truck, the driver gave him a blanket and helped Bruce wrap it around his shoulders. "Where are you going?" he asked.

"Home," Bruce said. The driver nodded and drove on, not asking any more questions. Bruce was grateful for this simple act of kindness.

Bruce got across the border from Guatemala into Mexico, and slumped exhausted in the main market of a small town in Chiapas. He had to rest. A boy put a few coins into his hand, thinking he was a beggar.

The coins didn't amount to much, but they were enough that he could get a shirt and a pair of pants at a nearby stall. The vendor gave him things in his size, but Bruce looked at the pants, thinking about what he would do if the Hulking Monster came back. He'd need something... "¿*Tienes más*... stretchy?" he asked, and the vendor smiled at his bad Spanish. But she found him a large, stretchy pair of pants. They were comically big on him, but they might hold together during a transformation.

Dressed again, Bruce felt better. He got something to eat, and then he kept going.

Blonsky walked with General Ross back into the command center at the Everglades base. "I've run into bad situations on crap missions before," he said. "I've seen good men go down purely because someone didn't let us know what we were walking into. I've moved on to the next one because that's what we do, right? I mean, that's the job. But this?" He stopped walking, and General Ross did, too. "This is a whole new level of weird," Blonsky said. "I don't feel inclined to step away from it. So if you're taking another crack at him, I want in."

He wanted to get back at Bruce for what had happened in the factory, but Blonsky also wanted more. He'd seen the creature's unthinkable power...and he wanted that, too.

"And with respect," he went on, "you should be looking for a team that's prepped and ready to fight. Because if that thing shows up again? You're going to have a lot of professional tough guys running for their mamas."

Blonsky could see Ross thinking, but all Ross did was dismiss him. It wasn't until a few days later that Ross called him in, and Blonsky got a whole new understanding of what they were up against.

"Let me emphasize that what I'm about to share with you is tremendously sensitive, both to me personally and to the army," Ross said as he and Blonsky walked through a hanger. It was filled with helicopters and armored vehicles. "You're aware that we've got an infantry weapons development program. Well, in World War Two, they initiated a subprogram for bio-tech force enhancement."

"Yeah, the Super-Soldier program," Blonsky said. He'd heard of it.

"Yes," Ross said. "An oversimplification, but yes. And I dusted it off, got them doing serious work again. Bold work. Across the hall, they were trying to arm you better.... We were trying to *make* you better."

"Banner's work was very early phase. It wasn't even weapons application. He thought he was working on radiation resistance." Ross smirked. "I would never have told him what the project really was. But he was so sure of what he was onto that he tested it on himself. And something went very wrong." His smirk changed to a real smile, the kind of smile someone got when they had a secret. "Or it went very right."

Ross started to get down to business now that he'd begun to let Blonsky in on the secrets of the Super-Soldier project. "As far as I'm concerned, that man's whole body is the property of the US Army."

"You said he wasn't working on weapons, right?" Blonsky asked.

"No."

"But you were, weren't you? You were trying other things."

Ross saw that Blonsky was starting to put two and two together. Good, he thought. Blonsky might be just what he was looking for. "One serum we developed," he said, "was very promising."

"So why did he run?" Blonsky asked.

Ross stood. "He's a scientist. He is not one of us. Blonsky, how old are you? Forty-five?"

Blonsky bristled but tried not to show it. "Thirty-nine," he said.

"It takes a toll, doesn't it?"

"Yes, it does."

"So get out of the trenches. You should be a colonel by now, with your record."

"No, I'm a fighter," Blonsky said. "I'll be one for as long as I can. You know, if I could take what I know now and put it in the body I had ten years ago, that would be someone I wouldn't want to fight."

Perfect, General Ross thought. He wants it. "I could probably arrange something like that," he said.

Recruiting was easy when you identified the right man for the job, he thought.

CHAPTER 9

Bruce headed toward the US border using any means of transportation he could find. He rode in the backs of trucks with migrant workers; climbed through hilly, rugged terrain; and hitchhiked whenever he could. When he couldn't find a ride, he grabbed some sleep—mostly outdoors or in the doorways of locked stores in small towns. He slept badly, plagued by nightmares of what had happened in the factory, but at least he was under the radar. In this way, he stayed one step ahead of Thunderbolt Ross...and he also stayed away from people as much as he could, fearing that the monster would get out again.

He'd started thinking of it as the Hulk. It was a separate thing from him, or at least he wanted it to be. If he gave it a name, that helped him keep it apart from the real Bruce Banner in his mind.

It took a long time for Bruce to travel through Central America and Mexico, but he finally reached the border of Texas. He crossed at night with a family of immigrants, helping the kids cross the rocky desert.

Then he made his way toward the East Coast, keeping to the smaller highways.

CHAPTER 10

Seventeen days after the incident in the Racinho Favela bottling plant, Bruce arrived at Culver University. After so long out of the country, a common-place sight like a college campus looked surprisingly foreign to him.

He strode over to a big stone building—the Maynard Hall of Physical Sciences—and watched the students and faculty enter and exit the hall. During a quiet moment, Bruce climbed up the stairs and peered through the entrance's window.

There was a checkpoint with a metal detector and a guard. Bruce knew he shouldn't be heading that way at all.

On the directory board, he saw a listing for *Cellular Biology—Dr. Elizabeth Ross.* Just seeing her name gave him chills, and Bruce hurried away.

He didn't go far. He sat on a bench, waiting.

Finally two women walked out of the building.

Bruce froze as he got his first look at Betty Ross in years. She was as beautiful as he remembered, although her hair was longer and bangs covered her forehead.

He watched as Betty got coffee with her friend from a cart. The women sat at a small table in the sunshine, then said good-bye after their break was over.

Bruce had an overwhelming urge to run to her, but before he could move, a man approached her with a smile. Betty smiled back, and they embraced. Bruce felt like he'd been punched in the stomach as they linked arms and walked away together.

She'd moved on. She'd forgotten him. Maybe she even thought he was dead.

Bruce walked to the edge of campus and spent the rest of the day wandering the city thinking of what he could do next. After nightfall, hungry and alone, he had an idea. He headed for one of his favorite off-campus hangouts, Stanley's Pizza. Stan, a thickset man in his early sixties, was an old friend. Just as Stan flipped over the sign on the door to CLOSED, Bruce knocked. Stan jumped like he'd seen a ghost and then opened the door.

The two old friends settled down to catch up at a table in a private back room. Stan brought pasta with his special sauce, and Bruce scarfed it down. He hadn't been eating much since he left Brazil.

"There've been so many rumors—" Stan started.

Bruce smiled. "Stan, I give you my word," he said, "whatever you've heard about me isn't true."

Stan patted Bruce's leg. "Oh, I know it. I always knew it. But you know how I felt about you two...Have you talked to—"

"No," Bruce replied, ducking his head sadly. "She doesn't know I'm here. She's with somebody?"

"His name's Leonard," Stan supplied. "He's a head shrink. They say one of the best. But a really nice guy. Reminds me of you a little... Sorry." Stan clapped his hands once, changing the subject. "Bruce, what can I do to help you?"

"I could use a place to stay for a few nights," Bruce said.

Stan opened his arms wide. "You can have the spare room upstairs."

"That'd be so great," Bruce said. He couldn't think of the last time he'd slept in a bed. "And there is, um... there is one other thing."

The next evening, Bruce set off on a bicycle, dressed in a Stanley's Pizza Parlor uniform, which included a T-shirt, hat, and sunglasses. After a few stops to deliver pizzas, he biked over to Maynard Hall and carried two pizzas up to the muscular guard at the lobby's security desk.

"Hey, pal, I got a delivery on five," Bruce told the guard.

The guard looked confused. "I don't think there's anybody up there."

Bruce let out a groan. "Oh man, I'm gonna be in so much trouble if I don't collect. You gotta let me try."

The guard didn't look impressed. "Tell you what," Bruce said. "I got an extra medium. Take it on the house."

The guard looked at the free pizza and thought about it, but just for a second. Then he nodded toward the elevators, letting Bruce through the checkpoint.

"You are the man," Bruce said, and got moving.

As he headed down the hallway toward his old lab, Bruce suddenly started to feel nervous. This was the place where the experiment had ruined his life. But maybe that could change. Maybe now it could be where he put his life back on track.

The setup had changed in the last five years. Bruce could see through the glass walls around the lab, that instead of physics equipment, it now held computer terminals, with large supercomputer arrays along the walls. A graduate student sat at a terminal, staring with bleary eyes.

Bruce opened the door. "Those jerks in radiation called this in and then split," he remarked, pointing at the pizza. "You want it?"

The graduate student smiled. "Whoever you are, you are my new personal hero."

Bruce glanced around at all the computers. "Hey," he asked, "you mind if I jump online for a second?"

"Totally, no problem," the student replied, already opening the pizza box.

"Righteous," Bruce said. He sat down at a terminal across from the student and quickly accessed the university's main system, which requested a username and password.

Bruce typed in "Dr. Elizabeth Ross" for the username and then was momentarily stumped for Betty's password. He tried "bettylovesbruce," which was rejected. Then he tried another old password of hers: "Cells_Unite!"

Bingo! He quickly looked for records of his experiment, but searching under both "USMD Research Protocol 456-72328" and "Gamma Pulse" yielded no results. Neither did a search on his own name.

He tried a few more searches before recognizing that no trace of the experiment existed at all in the system. The military must have had the records deleted completely! Bruce sagged in his chair, defeated. They had erased him. Officially, he didn't exist...but that wasn't going to stop General Ross from hunting him down. To Ross, all that mattered was the gamma powers the experiment had given Bruce.

The only thing he could think to do was take advantage of this brief moment of Internet access and get in touch with Mr. Blue. Quickly, Bruce started up the software that would let him run the encrypted chat program.

B: Mr. Green! How goes the search?
G: The data is gone.
B: Without it...I cannot help.

There was a pause, then Mr. Blue added:

B: So what now?
G: I've got to keep moving.

With a sigh, Bruce realized that there was nothing left for him in that lab. It was time to go.

CHAPTER 11

Bruce packed up and got ready to say good-bye to Stan. He didn't want to put his friend in danger by staying too long. Also, there was nothing at Culver University that was going to help with his cure. He had to stay moving so General Ross didn't find him before Bruce could at least get a sense of what his next step should be.

"We're pretty well closed here, folks, I'm sorry,"

he heard Stan say as he came down into the kitchen. Then he heard other voices and waited. As usual, Stan was willing to serve that one last customer who showed up late at the end of the night.

Something about one of the voices...Bruce went to the swinging kitchen doors and looked out into the dining area.

At that moment, Betty looked up over Leonard's shoulder to see who was there and gasped with shock. But then Leonard shifted his position, blocking her view. When he moved again, Bruce had vanished.

Leonard spoke, but Betty couldn't hear a word. She just stared through the swinging doors, and sprang past Leonard into the back room. "Bruce!" she yelled.

Bruce wasn't there, so Betty burst out the back door into an alley. Thunder rumbled in the distance as the first raindrops began to fall. Betty quickly glanced left and right. "Bruce!"

But there was no sign of him.

Little did Betty know, Bruce had flattened himself further behind a dumpster, holding his breath.

"Betty!" Leonard called as he followed her. "What's going on? Come inside." The rain was already falling harder.

Betty strode back inside, shaking, heading straight for Stan, who stood paralyzed behind the parlor counter. "Just tell me if I saw what I think I saw," Betty pleaded.

"Betty," Stan began, agonized between protecting Bruce and lying to an old friend. "I don't...know what to say."

Bruce was headed out of town. He didn't even know where. He walked along one of the main roads that led toward the closest interstate highway, trying to hitch-hike in the pouring rain. Nobody stopped...then, when he had just about resigned himself to another night spent walking in the rain, he heard a car pull to a stop behind him. Probably a policeman, Bruce thought, and started coming up with a good story. He also took a look around to see what the best escape route would be.

But when he turned around, he saw Betty getting out of her car, stunned at the sight of him. She had followed him, looked for him all over town probably, and knowing that made Bruce feel better than he'd felt in a long time.

She ran to Bruce and embraced him tightly. "Don't go," Betty begged. "I want you to come with me now. Please."

Bruce knew it wasn't safe. He knew he might be putting her in danger. But he couldn't help it, not with her right there talking to him, her arms wrapped around his neck and her heart beating fast.

Bruce hid in the back of Betty's car until they were inside the garage of the house she shared with Leonard. She went into the house first and pulled all the curtains so Bruce could move around unseen. Then, when he was sitting in the living room and dried off, she handed him a little jewel case. "It's our data," she said. "I got in there before they carted it all away. I hoped that it might tell us something someday."

Bruce looked at the tiny USB drive. It was such a little thing to have all his hopes for a cure inside it. "Does the general know you have this?"

"I don't think so," she said. "I haven't spoken to him in a couple of years."

"You have to be sure," he said.

"Bruce, I don't understand why we can't just go in there together and talk to him."

"He told me what he wanted to do. He wants it out of me. He wants to dissect it so that he can replicate it," Bruce said. He meant the monster, the Hulk. She knew about it. She had been there when it had first appeared. "He wants to make it a weapon."

After dinner, Betty led Bruce to a spare room. "Do you need anything?" she asked.

"No," he answered. "I should leave early. As early as I can."

"You can't stay at all?"

"I want to, but it's just not safe for me to be here. If I can borrow cash from you, I'll take the bus."

"Of course," Betty said quickly. "At least let me walk you to the station."

"Okay," Bruce said.

"You have everything you need?" she asked.

"Yeah," Bruce said. He didn't want her to leave, and he could tell she didn't want to, either. But they both said good night, and Bruce lay awake for a long time, wondering what tomorrow would bring.

General Ross picked up the serum from the secured medical storage rooms in the basement and took it upstairs to the lab, where two medical technicians were prepping for the procedure. Ross handed the canister to an assistant. Emil Blonsky, shirtless, came in, and Ross got right down to business.

"We're giving you a very low dose only. I need you sharp out there and disciplined," Ross said. "First sign of any side effects and you're off the team until you straighten out. Agreed?"

Blonsky nodded, committed to the path he'd chosen. "Agreed."

"You'll get two separate infusions, dripped in very slowly," a technician explained. "One deep into the muscle, one into the bone marrow centers." The tech smiled grimly. "The bone ones are going to hurt."

They put Blonsky on a table and strapped him in so they could keep him steady while they completed the injections. The first two went into the sides of his neck and weren't too bad.

Then they turned the table over. Hanging three feet over the floor facedown, Blonsky felt the technician's fingertips locating the right spot on his spine. The tech pressed down between two verbetrae.

A moment later, the needle went in, and it was the worst pain Blonsky had ever felt in his life. He'd seen combat. He'd been shot. Nothing had ever compared to this. He held himself back from screaming out loud only because he refused to give in to the pain. After what seemed like an eternity, the needle started to withdraw from his spine. As it did, Blonsky felt...

Different. Something was changing inside him.

And as the pain began to fade, he thought he was starting to feel...well...better than he had in a long time.

Still hung facedown, Blonsky smiled. It was not a pretty smile.

CHAPTER 12

When Bruce woke up in the morning, heavy thunder was rumbling in the distance. Another big storm was on the way. For the moment, though, it was a fine morning. Bruce and Betty walked together, cutting across campus toward the bus station. As they got to the library, Bruce stopped, looking around the quiet campus like something didn't feel right.

"Is everything okay?" Betty asked.

He came back to her and nodded. "I think so."

Bruce kept hitching at his pants, which were much too big for him. Betty watched him until she couldn't stand it anymore, and then she said, "Here."

Bruce stopped and Betty fixed his belt, cinching it tighter so it would hold up his pants. Bruce had been so distracted this hadn't occurred to him. "It's better like this," she said.

He smiled at her, but he was still nervous, looking all around. "Yeah? Thanks."

She pulled off his cap, adjusted its strap—an old habit of hers.

Bruce stared at her, chewing on his lip as she replaced his cap. Then his gaze shifted as he saw something over her shoulder.

"What is it?" Betty asked.

He grabbed Betty's shoulders. "Oh no," he groaned. "They're here."

"What—who—?" Betty sputtered.

"Betty, look at me. Look at me!" Bruce ordered. "You have to get as far away from me as you can! Don't argue with me, just go! Go!"

He broke away from her and bolted across the lawn.

CHAPTER 13

All along the lawn, soldiers exploded out from behind columns and trees, charging after Bruce.

Bruce sped into a sprint, weaving, desperate to out-distance the soldiers.

Hearing engines behind her, Betty spun around and gasped at the two huge vehicles roaring down the quad's perimeter. They smashed parked cars, splitting up and racing on either side of her—one bumping up on the grass, the other zooming down the road. One had a .50-caliber machine gun on its roof. Students scattered and got out their phones to take pictures of the chaotic scene.

Betty chased after the vehicles, trying to keep Bruce in sight.

He dashed off ahead of her, taking a hard turn down a columned walkway. The buildings opened up beyond a courtyard, into a field, and he bolted past that exit. Past the field, Bruce knew, was a large patch of forest.

On the monitors in their black van, General Ross and Major Sparr watched Bruce run. "Dammit, we'd have had snipers on target in three more minutes," Ross growled, furious that his trap had been sprung too soon. "I want to know who jumped the gun." He'd be handing down some discipline when this mission was completed.

Bruce whipped through a small grove of trees and reached the field, accelerating across the open ground. Along the edges of the field were the outer buildings of the campus—like the back of the library facility, which was connected to a performing arts center by a glassed-in overpass. Ahead of Bruce was a huge steel modern art sculpture.

Bruce veered slightly when vehicles appeared on the far edge of the performing arts center. From his new angle, he could see them motoring toward him from behind, followed by a group of soldiers on foot. He focused on the line of forest across the field—his only hope of escape.

Emil Blonsky outpaced the others like they were standing still, sprinting at an inhuman speed that brought him right up level with the automobiles as Bruce tore around the corner of the arts center and hurtled across a stone terrace. He sped toward the back doors of the library, burst inside, and raced down a narrow aisle between tall bookshelves.

Blonsky held up a clenched fist to stop the other soldiers from entering. "Look alive," he said. "This could get interesting."

His squad surrounded the building, and designated soldiers pursued Bruce inside.

When Betty neared the library, she stopped, taking in the swarm of soldiers around the building, with more pouring out of mobile transports and taking positions around the metal sculpture. Another team was sprinting from the forest. Far to the right were vehicles holding strange, bulky equipment. She spotted a black command van slowing near the transport and hustled toward it.

Inside the library, Bruce jumped up a narrow staircase and raced down another aisle, dropping to his knees between two shelves. He yanked the data flash card out of his pocket and removed its lanyard. Soldiers' footsteps clattered nearby, climbing the stairs toward him.

Bruce opened his mouth and shoved the data card down his throat. He forced himself to swallow it, coughing and gagging. There was no way he was going to lose the data again. No way. As soon as it was down, Bruce peeked out from behind a shelf, just as a soldier looked his way. The soldier yelled, and Bruce darted down the aisle.

Betty cut off the lead armored vehicle in a second group. She knew that's where the officers would be. "Stop! Stop!" she yelled, standing right in front of it. "I know you're in there! General, please!"

There was no response.

"Dad!" Betty screamed.

The van door opened, and her father stepped out. General Ross faced her impatiently, glancing over at the buildings. Two rangers guarded him from behind with their rifles.

"Please don't do this," Betty begged. "He needs help!"

"You can't see this clearly," Ross snapped at her. "Now get inside." He reached out to grab her arm, but she pulled away.

Bruce burst through the double doors of the overpass and into the glass-enclosed tube, running toward the performing arts center.

"There he is!" one of Ross's rangers shouted.

Everybody on the field watched Bruce bolting through the overpass. Above the buildings, ominous thunderclouds gathered, turning the sky a deep gray. A voice over a radio squawked, "Target is in the overpass. We have a visual."

"Do not engage," General Ross said into a walkie-talkie. "Repeat: Do not engage!"

When the commandos appeared on the side of the performing arts building, Bruce stopped short and spun around to run back to the library. But soldiers were waiting for him there, too. He stood in the middle of the overpass, trapped, his chest heaving, as he pondered his next move.

Ross tightened his hands to fists. "Put two canisters in there with him," he ordered. "One on either side."

The soldiers cornering Bruce quickly backed out and bolted the doors. Bruce stared at them in momentary confusion, but then he saw two missiles heading for the walkway. He ducked as small canisters broke through the glass. They clanked on the ceiling, clattered onto the floor, and then issued out clouds of thick smoke.

Bruce ripped off his shirt, then took a deep gasp of air and balled up the shirt over his nose and mouth.

"Bruce!" Betty screamed as she saw the tube fill with smoke. She broke away from her father and dashed toward the overpass.

"Get her back here!" Ross shouted, and his rangers scrambled after her.

Bruce's pulse raced, and he flailed around as he tried to stay in pockets of clean air. He pushed up against the glass, and his eyes widened when he saw a soldier reach Betty and grab her arm. She elbowed him and broke free. Bruce cried out as the other ranger tackled her to the ground.

Bruce dropped his shirt and pressed himself flat against the wall. Burning rage sizzled through his body, and his eyes flashed green. His chest heaved and contorted, his torso twisting as he tumbled back into the smoke.

Betty screamed as the smoke lit up with a flare of brilliant green.

In the van, all the radiation monitors spiked.

"The Geiger counter's lighting up!" Sparr yelled.

Ross didn't take his eyes off the smoke-filled overpass.

Neither did Emil Blonsky. His real target was about to arrive.

CHAPTER 14

Bruce contorted in the gas-filled passageway as the Hulk began to take over. Green energy shone in his eyes and surged from the base of his skull, gamma power flooding through his face and neck and shimmering in his arms. His feet split through his boots and his expanding body shredded his clothes.

Outside, Betty got to her knees, staring up at the overpass. A hand slapped onto the glass, clawing at it desperately. The hand glowed green, and its whole arm swelled, plumping with thick muscle before sliding back into the cloud of gas. The entire overpass seemed to vibrate with the sound of Bruce's anguished cries. When he fell silent, all anyone could see from the outside was a huge shadow, shifting in the gas as it rose and took the shape of—not a man, Betty thought. It was way too big to be just a man.

"Now she'll see," Ross said. Betty had thought her father was a monster, but she was about to see who the real monster was.

The shadow spread its massive arms and the whole center portion of the glass shattered at the impact of its fists. Tear gas poured out, and the soldiers could see the giant green creature, twice the height of a man and slabbed with muscle. Feral intelligence gleamed in his eyes. He snarled and leaped to the ground, trailing wisps of tear gas. When he landed, with one knee bent, Betty felt the impact in the ground under her feet.

The Hulk slowly rose to his full gargantuan height, and all the soldiers on the field took a step backward.

With three powerful strides, the Hulk cleared the courtyard, pounding toward the open field. He spotted Betty on the ground with General Ross beyond her, and he roared with rage, shaking his boulder-size fists in the air.

"Alpha Team, let him have all of it," Ross ordered.

A barrage of automatic weapons fire peppered the Hulk's right side, the bullets ricocheting off his skin in all directions. He flung up one arm and turned, seeing Alpha Team: six soldiers with assault rifles near the metal sculpture, arrayed around a tripod-mounted machine gun.

The Hulk raised his hand like a shield and charged toward the fire team. Another fusillade pounded into his palm and raked down his legs. But he didn't stop storming ahead. The soldiers scattered as he got closer.

Ross's rangers grabbed Betty, who was stunned by what she was seeing. Quickly, they hustled her away.

Ross swore softly, watching as the giant moved in the wrong direction. "Where are the .50-cals?" he roared. "Move!"

Two vehicles with roof-mounted .50-caliber machine

guns roared into view and accelerated to cut the Hulk off from his approach to the sculpture.

The first pulled up alongside the giant, and the gunner opened fire. The Hulk veered to his left, driving his shoulder into the vehicle and tipping it into a spectacular rolling crash. The roof gunner jumped free and tumbled across the grass. The second vehicle headed straight for him as he got closer to Alpha Team, still holding their position in and around the sculpture.

Hearing the vehicle's engine approach, the Hulk pivoted and stomped a foot down on its hood. It jacked up like a skateboard, its front wheels and bumper driven into the ground.

The Hulk heaved it into the air, shaking the soldiers loose. He smashed the wrecked vehicle into the sculpture, tearing it to pieces. Its engine fell near his feet. Thunder cracked across the sky as the Hulk roared and flung the engine at the other line of vehicles, smashing them into one another in a giant explosion.

"Blonsky! Now you're up!" Ross barked.

"Cover me," Blonsky said. He shouldered a grenade launcher and marched steadily toward the monster, firing as soon as he was clear of his own lines. The first grenade hit the creature square in the the back of his head, and he roared in surprise when it exploded. Then another detonated against the backs of his legs. But even though the grenades rocked the giant, they didn't take him down.

Peppered by bullets ricocheting off his enormous back, the giant snapped off one of the sculpture's large steel plates. He held its center bolt like the handle of a huge shield. Then he tore a second plate loose, the sound of popping rivets echoing between gunshots from Ross's retreating forces.

He held up both metal plates, shaking them angrily in the air and clashing them together in a challenge to Blonsky, who fired another grenade and watched the creature duck behind the makeshift shields. Then he looked around the edge, green eyes burning with fury.

"Remember me?" Blonsky asked.

The creature roared and charged, hacking at Blonsky with the metal plates and trying to pin him to the ground. But Blonsky was feeling the Super-Soldier formula. He dodged the scything sheets of metal and fired his pistol when he ran out of grenades. The bullets weren't going to hurt the green giant, but that wasn't the plan. Blonsky was trying to lead him on a chase.

"He's doing it!" Ross said from the mobile command post, a larger version of the van they'd used in Brazil. It was incredible to see. A battlefield-ready Super-Soldier! This was the kind of moment Ross had been building toward for his entire career. It even eased the sting of Banner's disastrous failure . . . a little.

"Move him toward the cannons!" he shouted.

Ahead of Blonsky appeared two vehicles tearing through the woods to the edge of the field. They skidded to a halt fifty yards apart. On each was a massive conical sound projector—another of Ross's research projects.

With another burst of speed, Blonsky dashed into the speakers' range, with the creature hot on his tail.

The soldiers operating the speakers hesitated, unsure if they should fire with Blonsky in the way.

"Do it now!" Blonsky howled.

The operators fired the sonic cannons, unleashing low-frequency sound loud enough that the waves of it rippled visibly in the air.

The edge of the sonic blast caught Blonsky and flung him aside. He rolled when he hit the ground and popped back up to watch the fireworks.

The overlapping sound waves converged on the Hulk, stopping him in his tracks. He roared in agony and dropped his makeshift shields to clap his hands over his ears.

Blasting beyond the Hulk, the sonic waves split trees and shattered windows.

The Hulk's suffering bellows were barely audible over the basso thunder of the sound projectors. He crouched down, dark green blood trickling from his ears, and dropped to his knees, trying to hold himself upright. Clearly the sound was doing more damage than machine guns could.

"Please, please, no!" Betty begged her father, and she broke free of the soldiers guarding her to grab the front of his uniform.

"Get her back," General Ross ordered.

As the soldiers dragged Betty away, she screamed, "You're killing him!"

CHAPTER 15

etty broke free from the soldiers' clutches and sprinted across the field. The rangers bolted after her. They caught Betty, holding her fast.

She strained against their grip. "Bruce!" she screamed.

A confused look crossed the giant's face at the sound of that name. Then he seemed to recognize her. He shuddered, and a green pulse flared, surging out from his skull.

Slowly, the Hulk got up, bracing himself with the steel

sculpture pieces. When he reached his feet, he roared a challenge to the sound projectors, smashing the shields together like giant cymbals. The crash countered the sonic waves for just a moment—and that was all it took for the Hulk to fling one plate discus-style at the left-hand sound projector. It split the projector cone in half and careened away into the trees.

The sound waves from the right cannon refocused, but the Hulk held up his remaining shield and leaned into the sonic blast, driving himself forward step by step. Ross's soldiers resumed small-arms fire but the barrage did not distract the Hulk this time. He stayed focused on the sound projector, and when he got close enough, he leaped up and put all his weight into a downward blow with the flat of the metal shield.

The impact crushed the rear of the automobile flat. In the silence, he turned to find Betty... but instead saw a furious Thunderbolt Ross.

"Where is my gunship?" he barked.

None of the soldiers moved as the Hulk stared them down. They'd thrown everything they had at him and had barely left a mark. Only Blonsky, riding the wave of his newfound Super-Soldier strength, dared to act. Angling around behind the Hulk, he emptied a full clip from an AR-15 into Hulk's back.

The Hulk slowly turned around to face him, staring down at Blonsky, who stared right back.

"Is that it?" Blonsky asked, taunting him.

"Blonsky, pull back now!" Ross ordered over the radio.

The Hulk's eyes narrowed with hatred. He twitched his giant shield as though he might swing it. *That's right*, Blonsky thought. *You recognize me, don't you? But I'm not the same as I was before.*

"Come on," he said. Not wanting to be bothered with more orders he would just ignore, he pulled out the earpiece that kept him in contact with Ross. Still looking the Hulk in the eye, he said, "Is that all you've got?"

For a moment, the Hulk studied Blonsky. Then...

Smash! The Hulk raised one foot and drove it into Blonsky heel-first with a gruesome crunch. The impact sent Blonsky straight back into the trunk of an oak tree. He hit it hard enough to shake leaves from its branches, and then his body fell limp to the grass.

Ross's jaw clenched in dismay. Apparently the Super-Soldier program still needed some refinements.

Lightning cracked across the dark sky, and it started to rain as the the Hulk stomped over to Betty.

"Fall back!" Ross ordered his troops. "Find cover!" The command echoed down the line, and the soldiers began to fall back toward the tree line.

Betty stepped closer to the Hulk as an Apache helicopter hove into view over the line of trees across from the destroyed pedestrian overpass. It cleared the trees and dropped into a hover, locking onto the Hulk...whose bulk blocked Betty from the pilot's view.

She raised her hand to touch the Hulk's giant green arm. "Bruce?" she whispered.

The Hulk heard his name over the *thup-thup-thup* of the Apache's rotors. A spark of recognition flashed in his eyes.

As Ross and Sparr coordinated the retreat, Sparr glanced back to check the progress of the rangers who had been holding Betty. They were headed across a road toward cover on the far side...without Betty.

Looking back toward the field, Sparr spotted Betty standing with the Hulk just as Ross—who didn't seem to notice where his daughter was—gave the Apache's pilot the order to fire.

"Hold on to your hats," the pilot replied.

Sparr waved her arms frantically. "Hold fire!" she screamed.

But it was too late. The Apache's twin rotating cannons unloaded, tearing up the earth around Betty and the Hulk.

Betty instinctively pressed her body against him for shelter as cannon shells pounded into the Hulk's back, the flesh of his legs, the skin over his shoulder blades. Keeping Betty behind him, he wheeled around to face the onslaught.

The gunship accelerated toward him, continuing its strafing run. When it was too close to take evasive action, the Hulk sidearmed the remaining piece of the sculpture at it. The sheet metal ripped through the gunship's main rotor mount and the helicopter nosed down into an uncontrolled plunge. Its crew jumped out as it plowed into the ground and started to roll, sparks showering from shredded electrical conduits. The Hulk grabbed Betty and wrapped himself around her for protection as he turned his back to the tumbling aircraft. The helicopter exploded as it rolled, engulfing the giant in flames.

The force of the blast knocked everyone nearby to the ground. Ross raised his head, staring at the inferno and understanding only now what he had done. There was no way his daughter could have survived the blast.

But then the Hulk stepped out of the flames, his face contorted with pain and cradling Betty in his arms. Lightning split the sky as rain poured down, spitting in the flaming wreckage of the Apache. The Hulk, wreathed in fire, sheltering Betty against his massive chest, stood snarling at Ross.

A crack of thunder boomed, and the Hulk began to run. He gathered speed as he crossed the field, past the soldiers and the wreckage, past Blonsky's crumpled body. Ross and Sparr could only watch as he ran with Betty and disappeared into the darkness of the forest.

CHAPTER 16

In the aftermath of the disastrous attempt to capture the Hulk, General Ross stood on Leonard's porch, hoping Betty's boyfriend might be able to help him find Bruce...and Betty. After all, he was the one who had alerted General Ross that Bruce was in the area.

"You did the right thing, calling us," Ross said.

Leonard didn't look convinced.

"I need to know where they're going," Ross said. A group of soldiers came out of the house with boxes of material seized for Ross's investigation. Anything in the house that might be a clue to Bruce's location was going back to the base for analysis.

"She'll be in incredible danger as long as she's with him," Ross said.

"From who?" Leonard shot back. "He protected her. You almost killed her."

Ross wanted to grab the doctor and shake him until the answers fell out, but he held himself back. "I give you my word, her safety is my main concern at this point."

Showing courage Ross wouldn't have expected from a man who spent his days behind a desk, Leonard stood up and got right in Ross's face. "You know, it's a point of professional pride for me that I can always tell when someone is lying," he said. "And you are. I don't know where he's going. I know she'll help him if she can."

"Then she's aiding a fugitive, and I can't help either of them," Ross said. He wasn't going to get anything more out of the psychiatrist. He stood to leave. There were more important things to do.

"I used to wonder why she never talked about you," Leonard called as Ross strode through the rain toward his car. "Now I know."

Ross rolled his eyes. "Where does she meet these guys?" he grumbled.

Through a raging storm, the Hulk crashed deep into the forest, pushing his way through the trees for hours until he reached the base of the Smoky Mountains. He climbed the foothills, and then spotted a cave opening in the jagged rocks.

He extended his arms into the cave, gently laying Betty down in a dry spot.

As soon as he let go, Betty startled awake. She gasped, confused when she saw the monstrous face. Betty let out a scream. He jerked back, and his head cracked into the roof of the cave.

The creature growled, surprised by the pain.

"Oh no," Betty moaned, realizing who he was. "I'm sorry."

The Hulk stood by the entrance of the cave; he couldn't fit inside fully.

Betty wrapped her arms around herself in the cold cave. She took her purse strap off her shoulder and removed her wet raincoat, shaking it out and then draping it over herself like a blanket. She looked up at the Hulk.

He pulled away, groaning. In his vision, Betty looked warped and distorted, bizarrely fractured in two. The sound of rain sizzled, like acid.

"Bruce, can you understand me?" Betty asked.

Her voice soothed him, and he settled down for a second—until a bright flash of lightning exploded in the sky.

The creature roared; the blast terrified and enraged him. He whipped around, searching for the source of the attack. When lightning flickered again, he grabbed a boulder and hurled it at the sky. She realized he was trying to protect her against what he thought was a menace from the clouds.

"It's okay!" Betty called to him. "We're okay." She stepped out of the cave into the rain, then touched the creature gently on his arm.

He turned abruptly, growling at her, but Betty wasn't afraid. She put her hand on one of his fingers and peered at his arm. "Come here," she said soothingly, inviting him to sit beside her under the cave's overhanging ledge. "Come this way. Watch your head." She gave him a tug, and he sat down beside her, out of the rain.

"We're okay," she said. "It's okay. It's just the rain." She knew Bruce was in there somewhere. The fact that the green giant had protected her told her that much. But the experiment had done something awful—and incredible—to him, and Betty had no idea how they might reverse it. Or, she thought as she watched the creature relax and gaze out into the rainy night, even how to control it.

Ross strode into the army hospital and caught up with a doctor. "Will Blonsky walk again?" he demanded to know.

The doctor stopped short. "Most of his bones look

like crushed gravel right now," he replied. "I will say this for him. He's got a heart like a machine. Never seen anything like it outside of a racehorse."

Ross winced as he followed the doctor into Blonsky's intensive care room. The soldier was bandaged from head to toe, with every machine imaginable hooked up to him.

The fact that Blonsky was still alive meant the formula had done something. On the other hand, the fact that he was this badly hurt meant the formula hadn't done enough. Ross had some tweaking to do before the next time he used a human subject. He left to return to the lab—and to check on the search for Betty.

In the morning, Betty woke up to find Bruce sleeping beside her.

She sat up quietly and stared at him. He looked exhausted and weak, but his skin was smooth—all his wounds had healed completely.

When he woke, Bruce felt sick and miserable. They couldn't stay up in the cave, though. They had to get moving. It took them all day, but they made their way down out of the mountains to a small town with a motel. Betty rented a room while Bruce hid behind an ice machine, wearing her raincoat and his shredded pants.

Betty helped him into the room, then left to buy supplies while he showered.

When she came back with shopping bags, Betty heard Bruce vomiting in the bathroom.

She put down her purchases on the bed and waited, concerned.

Bruce finally emerged from the bathroom with a toothbrush stuck in the corner of his mouth, not looking as bad as Betty feared. He was still wet from the shower. "Oh, hi," he said.

"You okay?" she asked.

"Yeah, I feel better actually," he replied. He held up the thumb drive she had saved from the old lab. "I just had to get my data back."

Betty was glad to see it. On that drive was their

only chance to control the gamma radiation in Bruce's blood. But still... "You *ate* it?"

"Yeah," Bruce said sheepishly. "The circumstances called for a little improvisation."

"Wow," Betty said. She pointed toward the bed. "Okay, so they didn't have a great selection, but I got you a few options. First things first."

She pulled a small box out of the bag and tossed it to him.

Bruce glanced down at a pulse monitor. "You're kidding me."

"Okay, now, it's no Armani, but..." Betty began to pull clothes out of the bags, holding them up so he could see the sizes. Most were too small, and he gave those the thumbs-down. Then she tossed him a pair of stretchy purple pants.

He held them up to his waist. Then he shot her a look.

Betty couldn't help but laugh. "What? They were the stretchiest ones they had!"

"I'll take my chances," he said, sitting down on the bed beside her.

After he'd chosen a different pair of pants, Betty gave Bruce a haircut, which he sorely needed. "You've done this on your own for all this time," she said as she ran her fingers through his hair.

"Usually with clippers," he joked, but they both knew she meant more than just haircuts.

They laughed, and soon they were kissing. Bruce wanted to tell her about all the times he'd thought of her during the last five years, but with her right there, none of that mattered. He had her back.

He broke the kiss as his heart rate started to speed up. "Whoa," he said. "I can't get too excited."

"Not even a little excited?" she asked with a playful pout. He sighed and rested his head against her chest. She stroked his hair. "It's okay," she said.

They sat together and started to talk about what they were going to do next.

CHAPTER 17

Ross paced across his office as he watched the news reports on TV. He grimaced as they showed footage of the final explosion.

The coverage switched to a reporter in a newsroom. "Rumors continue to swirl about a clash between the US military and an unknown adversary at Culver University earlier today," the reporter announced.

The TV now showed a blond reporter standing with two students on campus. "Very few outside the military got a firsthand look at who—or what—the soldiers were fighting," she said. "Sophomores Jack McGhee and Jim Wilson were coming home from a hike and witnessed some of the battle. McGhee captured this on his cell phone." The screen flashed an extremely grainy image of the creature.

The reporter held up her microphone to the nearest student, Jack McGhee. "Can you describe what you saw?" she asked.

"Dude, it was huge and green!" McGhee exclaimed.

"Dude, it was so big," Wilson agreed. "It was like this huge...hulk."

The reporter faced the camera again. "Further search for the mysterious 'hulk' was delayed by powerful thunderstorms in Smoky Mountains National Park."

Ross wheeled around when Sparr entered his office.

"Sir. It's Blonsky," said Sparr.

Ross and Sparr hustled toward the hospital ward. As they pushed through the ICU doors, Ross asked, "Has anybody found out if he had next of kin or family?"

Sparr held open the door for him. "You can ask him yourself," she replied.

A group of doctors and nurses backed away from Blonsky's bed as Ross entered, and Ross could see Blonsky sitting up, laughing. One of the nurses was taking off a metal splint from his hand. He was completely healed. Ross reconsidered what he'd thought earlier about the Super-Soldier serum. Apparently it had made Blonsky tougher than Ross had thought.

Blonsky grinned when he saw Ross. "Sir," he said.

Ross approached Blonsky and looked him over, astounded by the recovery. There wasn't a mark on him, and considering what Blonsky had looked like when they'd medevacked him back here, that was nothing short of incredible. "Good to see you back on your feet, soldier."

"Thank you, sir," Blonsky said.

Ross kept looking at him, gauging his health from how Blonsky sat, how his eyes tracked everything in the room...and how the smile on his face didn't really hide the expression of a man who wanted revenge. "How do you feel?" Ross asked.

Blonsky's grin widened. "Ready for round three," he replied.

Betty emptied the contents of her purse onto the motel bedspread. She had a phone, a credit and debit card, her driver's license, forty dollars in cash, some makeup, her university ID, and a digital camera.

Betty shrugged. "I thought if you asked me to go, I ought to be ready."

Bruce smiled, touched that she was prepared to join him. He collected everything from the bedspread except the money and the camera, and put them back into her purse. "Basically we can't use any of this because they can track all of it," he said.

"How about my lip gloss?" Betty joked. "Can they track that?"

With a laugh, Bruce said, "No, you can keep that."

"And I need my glasses," she added.

"You can—" Bruce stopped as he realized she was having fun with him. "We can use most of it," he corrected himself. "We just can't use the credit cards, the ID, or the phone. Don't even turn the phone on."

Betty looked down at the money in his hand. "How will we get where we need to go on forty dollars and no credit cards?"

Bruce looked down at the floor. He didn't have an answer for her.

"We can sell this," Betty said. She removed a chain from her neck, pulling up a lovely gold pendant. Bruce knew she had gotten it as an inheritance from her mother.

"No," Bruce said firmly. "It's the only thing you have left from her. No."

"Well, we'll have to try to get it back," Betty said.

In that moment, Bruce realized how lucky he was to have her on his side.

Ross stood in the Pentagon planning room, looking over the team he had assembled as Sparr wrapped up the briefing on the Banner situation. They all stared up at Bruce's and Betty's photos on the projection screen.

"Federal is already monitoring phone, plastic, and Dr. Ross's Web accounts, and local police have been on alert," Sparr continued. "They'll pop up somewhere, and when they do, it comes straight to us."

Ross cleared his throat. "They're not gonna just pop up," he interjected. "Banner made it five years and got across borders without making a mistake. He won't use a credit card now. If he was trying to escape, he'd be long gone. He's not trying to disappear this time—he's looking for help." The general raised a hand and closed it into a fist. "*That's* how we're going to get him. We know what they're after, and we know he's been talking to somebody. You all have copies of the correspondence. The aliases Mr. Green and Mr. Blue have been added to the S.H.I.E.L.D. Operations Database. If he comes up for air, we'll be waiting. If he makes a peep, we'll hear him. And when he slips up, we'll be ready."

Betty counted out cash to the young guy working at the counter at a gas station. While the clerk was distracted, Bruce stepped into the attached garage and spotted a greasy-looking computer terminal on a desk. He plugged the USB drive into the computer.

He didn't have time to download the chat software, and also he couldn't attach files that way. Mr. Blue needed data, and Mr. Green wanted him to have it. So Bruce typed a quick e-mail to an address at Grayburn College, where he knew Mr. Blue worked. He used a subject line guaranteed to get Mr. Blue's attention: *File from Mr. Green.*

The message was simple. *Mr. Blue. Here's the data. It's time to meet. —Mr. Green.* Then he uploaded the data from the drive and sent it off.

Betty came out of the store as he exited the garage. She held up a set of keys and smiled, pointing at a battered pickup truck. As Bruce removed the FOR SALE sign from the window and tossed it in the back of the truck, Betty said, "Hey..."

Bruce faced her, then grimaced when he saw her holding up the camera.

"It's been worse than this before, right?" Betty asked.

"Yes," Bruce replied. "Much worse."

"And you're not just running now," Betty continued. "We're on the way to something better. So smile."

Bruce tried, but he was afraid he didn't give her much of a smile to work with. But she snapped the picture anyway.

They were still on the highway as night fell. Betty drove, and Bruce leaned his head against the passenger-side window.

Betty took a deep breath. "What is it like?" she asked. "When it happens, what do you experience?"

"Remember those experiments we volunteered for at Harvard? Those induced hallucinations? It's a lot like that. Just a thousand times amplified. It's like someone's poured a liter of acid into my brain."

It was a scary thing to hear, but Betty went on. She loved Bruce and wanted him to know that she was with him for whatever he needed her to hear, and whatever he needed her to do. "Do you remember anything?" she asked.

"Just fragments. Images. There's too much noise. I can never derive much out of it."

"But then it's still you...inside him," Betty said.

"No. No, it's not," Bruce responded curtly.

Betty let that sit before replying. "I don't know," she began. "In the cave, I really felt like it knew me. Maybe your mind is in there, it's just overcharged and can't process what's happening."

"I don't want to control it. I want to get rid of it," Bruce said sullenly.

Betty wanted to say more, but she could tell Bruce was shutting down. He couldn't come to grips with the creature inside him, and Betty knew if she was in his shoes she would probably have had the same trouble. Bruce turned away from her, staring out the window into the darkness.

All he could see was his own reflection.

CHAPTER 18

In a secret medical lab, Blonsky sat back on a hospital bed. Two nearby technicians prepared syringes of Super-Soldier serum, while another one hooked Blonsky up to monitors.

Ross stepped up to the edge of the bed. "You ready?" he asked.

Blonsky smiled. "Let's even the playing field a little," he replied.

In her office in a building across the base from the medical facility, Major Sparr looked up. S.H.I.E.L.D.'s search computer had turned up a hit on the term "Mr. Blue."

She clicked on the result and ran down all possible avenues. Got him, she thought. This had to be the guy Bruce was going to see.

Bruce woke up in the truck sometime in the afternoon. They were inching down the highway in heavy traffic, and he couldn't tell how long he'd been asleep. On the radio, an announcer softly recited the news. "Bruce, wake up," Betty said. "There's something going on."

Bruce peered out the front windshield at the traffic jam. The reporter on the radio mentioned traffic delays due to a heightened security alert, and Bruce opened his door and looked out. Far ahead, he could see the gates of a toll booth at the entrance of the Holland Tunnel. Uniformed officers stood by the gates, staring at faces in the cars slowly passing by the checkpoint.

"We've got to go," Bruce decided.

Betty glanced at him in alarm.

"Walk toward the back," Bruce said. "Just don't move too fast."

Both of them exited the truck, abandoning it on the road. Picking their way through the slow lines of honking cars, they headed for the shoulder and hiked down a gravelly slope.

They made their way through an industrial area of Jersey City to the edge of the Hudson River. There Bruce spotted a dock in the distance. They approached one of the fishermen, a tall guy with a mop of gray hair who was leaning against a railing with a fishing pole. Betty chatted with him, offering him some money. The fisherman nodded.

A few minutes later, they took a seat in a small

outboard motorboat. The fisherman throttled the engine, and Bruce and Betty faced forward as they puttered out onto the river. The Statue of Liberty and New York City shimmered in the sunlight across the water.

They docked near Battery Park, thanked the fisherman, and walked up onto the streets of the city. Ten or fifteen minutes later, they'd gotten as far as Chambers Street. Betty and Bruce stopped by a map kiosk to figure out the best route to their destination.

"It's a long way uptown," Betty pointed out. "I think the subway's probably quickest."

Bruce chuckled. "Me in a crowded metal tube underground with hundreds of other people in the most aggressive city in the world?"

"Right," said Betty. "Let's get a cab."

The cab driver who picked them up was easily the most reckless driver in a city full of reckless drivers.

Betty gasped as the taxi slashed wildly across two lanes on Sixth Avenue. The driver slammed on the breaks randomly, honked his horn every few seconds, nearly killed a bike messenger, and sped through yellow lights instead of slowing down for them. The radio blared music while the driver jabbered on his cell phone. Bruce and Betty slammed around in the back-seat.

Bruce's new pulse monitor beeped as his heart rate climbed past ninety-seven beats per minute...up to ninety-eight...then ninety-nine...

He put his head back and closed his eyes, breathing deeply.

The cab screeched to a halt near Columbus Circle, in midtown Manhattan, bumping into the curb by an entrance to Central Park. They weren't close to their destination, but they couldn't stand that insane ride any longer!

Betty chucked a few bills through the passenger-side window. "Are you out of your mind! That was the worst cab ride I've ever had!" she yelled.

The driver just made a kissing noise and screeched away.

Betty kicked the rear bumper as it passed her. "Jerk!" she yelled, letting out all her pent-up frustration.

"You know," Bruce suggested softly, "I know a few techniques that could help you manage that anger very effectively."

"You zip it," Betty snapped. "We're walking."

"Okay," Bruce said.

CHAPTER 19

Outside Grayburn College's science building, Professor Sterns walked down the front steps, shuffling a stack of papers in his hands.

Betty hurried over to him. "Excuse me, Dr. Sterns?" she said. "Sorry to bother you, I'm Elizabeth Ross."

Dr. Sterns stared at her in surprise. "Oh! Dr. Ross!" he replied with a gasp. "I devoured your paper on synthesizing myostatin! To what do I owe the pleasure?"

Betty waved to Bruce, who strode up the stairs to join them. "I have someone who would like to meet you," Betty said.

"Okay," Sterns said as Bruce approached.

Bruce stuck out his hand for the professor to shake. "It's Mr. Blue, isn't it?"

Dr. Stern's mouth dropped open. "Mr. Green!"

Up in Dr. Sterns's office, Bruce and Betty stepped through a mad scientist's clutter of books, papers, chemical models, and scientific equipment. There was nowhere for guests to sit, so they stood in front of the professor's messy desk.

Dr. Sterns plopped down in his desk chair, chattering away happily. "I've got to tell you, I've been wondering if you were even real," he said. "And if you were, what would it look like? A person with that much power lurking in him. Nothing could have surprised me more than this unassuming man shaking my hand. But look, we're not strolling into the park for a picnic here. Even if everything goes perfectly, if we induce an episode, if we get the dosage exactly right...is that going to be a lasting cure, or just some antidote to suppress that specific flare-up?" He mimed flipping a coin. "I don't know."

Sterns's expression grew serious. "What I'm saying is if we overshoot by even a small integer... These concentrations carry extraordinary levels of toxicity."

"You mean it could kill him," Betty translated.

"Kill him? Yeah," Sterns agreed. "I should say so."

Betty and Bruce glanced at each other. It sounded like a big decision to make, but Bruce would try anything if it meant never losing control to the Hulk again.

"You should know that there's a flip side to this, too," Bruce said. "If we miss on the low side—if we induce me and the antidote fails—it will be very dangerous for you," he warned them.

Dr. Sterns chuckled and shrugged off the warning. "Look. I've always been far more curious than cautious," he said. "And that's served me pretty well." He clapped his hands together abruptly. "So. Are we going to do this?"

Betty and Bruce both nodded.

"Into the glorious unknown!" Dr. Sterns cheered.

At the Everglades base, helicopters were staging for the operation to take down Bruce. Flight crews did their final checks and ground support techs checked boxes on their mission-prep lists.

Inside the barracks, Blonsky stood alone in a locker room, staring at himself in the mirror. He still looked as he always had—a smallish man, compact in build, not too muscular. He was the kind of men others always underestimated, until they came up against him in a fight.

But now, as he watched, his body began to change. The new dose of the Super-Soldier serum was taking hold. Blonsky watched, and he liked what he saw. It hurt, but nothing worth having was ever painless. And this? Oh yes. It was worth having.

Blonsky grinned crazily at himself in the mirror.

A few hours later, he boarded a high-tech helicopter with a troop of other special forces soldiers. Besides him, there were three two-man shooting teams.

Thermal scopes and rifles were racked against the wall.

Blonsky sat across from a soldier who had been in the Culver University battle.

"How you feeling, man?" the soldier asked him.

"Like a monster," Blonsky replied with a grin.

CHAPTER 20

r. Sterns and Betty prepared Bruce's experimental procedure. Betty thought that the lab table looked disturbingly like a prison bed for administering lethal injections. The whole laboratory had a Dr. Frankenstein vibe that made her feel unnerved.

Bruce stripped to his stretchy Lycra shorts and handed his clothes to Betty. "Think of all the money I'll save on wardrobe if this works," he joked. When she didn't laugh, his expression grew solemn. "If this starts to go bad," he said, "promise me you won't try to help."

"Bruce—" Betty began.

"It's the worst when it starts," he interrupted. "You have to promise me you'll run or I can't do this."

Betty nodded.

"Okay. On the table," Dr. Sterns said. He pointed to the medical restraints on the lab table. "If you have a strong reaction, these will keep you from hurting yourself."

Bruce chuckled. He climbed up onto the table and lay down. "You can tell me later if you thought it was strong."

Dr. Sterns tilted the table back and attached the straps to Bruce's wrists and ankles. Betty helped him insert an IV linked to the cell saturation machine into each of Bruce's arms and legs. Dr. Sterns opened a canister containing the antidote and connected it to a plunger attached to the IV tubes. He pounded on one of the machines, saying something about his graduate students messing it up. Finally, Dr. Sterns stuck contact pads connected to electrical wires onto Bruce's temples.

"This will be a somewhat novel sensation," he said. He was flying high, ready to conduct the experiment of his professional lifetime. Bruce seemed calm. Betty was nervous—scared, in fact—but trying to keep a cool demeanor.

Dr. Sterns pressed the switch and said, "We have begun. The dialysis machine will mix the antidote with your blood, except the antidote will only take hold once we've achieved a full reaction."

The IV tubes filled with a swirling mixture of Bruce's blood and the bluish antidote fluid.

"Just relax," Betty said. Bruce was breathing hard, but she couldn't tell exactly what he was feeling.

"Okay, we are comprehensive," Dr. Sterns said. He handed Betty a bite guard, and she put it in Bruce's mouth. Then Dr. Sterns positioned himself at Bruce's head with a set of shock pads.

"All right," he said. "We set to pop?"

Bruce looked at Betty. Sterns noticed they were

holding hands and said to Betty, "I'd take your hands off him."

She did.

Bruce was jolted with electricity. His body bucked with uncontrollable spasms, his muscles straining against the straps, his eyes clenched shut.

Then Bruce's eyes snapped open, glowing with an intense green light.

The pulse of vibrant green flashed in the base of Bruce's skull, and green gamma energy coursed through his body as his skin flooded with color.

"My goodness!" Dr. Sterns blurted. He started to shut the procedure down, thinking it was complete.

"Wait, wait! There's more," Betty warned.

Bruce writhed as the full force of the transformation hit him, and his muscles swelled, stretched, and hardened. His bones cracked as they adjusted to his new shape.

Betty winced as Bruce howled with pain. Sterns covered his mouth, staggered by the changes. He stepped closer.

The restraints popped, like rubber bands, around

Bruce's thickening wrists. One strap slapped Dr. Sterns in the face, knocking him back as the Hulk appeared on the table, still shuddering with pain.

"Now!" Betty yelled. "Do it!"

The lab table buckled under the giant's weight. He raised his head, growling, his eyes filled with rage.

Betty jumped up onto the table and leaned against the creature's torso, staring directly into his furious green eyes. "Bruce. Bruce, look at me. Stay with me!" Betty said.

He just roared.

"The antidote—now! Sterns, do it now!" Betty screamed.

Sterns turned back to the monitors controlling the experiment. "Bruce, look in my eyes," Betty said, trying to soothe him.

"Oh, you've got to be kidding me," Sterns said. He ran and kicked the machine holding the canister of antidote fluid. With a whine, it started up, and the antidote started to flow down the tubes.

For a long moment, it seemed to have no effect. But then, miraculously, the process started to reverse itself!

The antidote flowed through the giant's veins, calming the radiation fire in his blood. The Hulk dwindled, and eventually he was gone; all that remained was a shivering, tired Bruce.

Still kneeling above him, Betty stroked Bruce's forehead. "Bruce, can you hear me?" she whispered. She said his name again. He was drenched with sweat. "It's okay," Betty whispered. "You're okay. You did it."

"He's fine," Dr. Sterns said, amazed at what he was seeing on the monitors. "This is fantastic."

"It's over," Betty said.

Bruce got his eyes focused on her. "Hi," he said.

She smiled. "Hi."

After Bruce felt well enough to discuss the experiment, Dr. Sterns gave his take on how it had gone. He was even more animated than he had been before they'd started. "That was the most extraordinary thing I have seen in my entire life!"

"Okay, you know what? Stop, please," Betty cut in.

"We need to go back and talk about what just happened in there."

"Absolutely. Okay. The gamma pulse came from the amygdala," Dr. Sterns said, hammering out combinations of keystrokes at a nearby terminal. "I think Dr. Ross's primer lets the cells absorb the energy temporarily, and then it abates." Looking at Bruce, he added, "That's why you didn't die of radiation sickness years ago. Now maybe we've neutralized those cells permanently or maybe we just suppressed that event," Sterns said rapidly. "I'm inclined to think the latter, but it's hard to know because none of our test subjects survived.... Of course, they weren't getting the primer!"

Bruce sat up. "Wait, wait. What did you just say?"

"They weren't getting the myostatin primer," Sterns said.

"No, no, no. Test subjects?" This was the first Bruce had ever heard of this. "What test subjects?"

Dr. Sterns jumped up and said, "Come with me."

Flanked by New York Police Department cars, Ross's team arrived at the perimeter of the Grayburn College campus and deployed.

Sniper teams took roof positions around the Grayburn College lab building. Each team consisted of one shooter and one spotter with a thermal scanner.

In the command van nearby, Ross and Sparr watched as their monitors lit up with readouts from those scanners—thermal images of Betty, Bruce, and Sterns moving through the lab.

"Target is the tallest," Sparr told the snipers. "Standing in the middle."

Downstairs in the Grayburn science building, a NYPD SWAT officer hustled a chunky security guard out of the lobby, and Blonsky and his team marched into position by the elevators.

"We still don't know which was more toxic, the gamma or your blood," Sterns was saying as he led them into a different room next to his lab. It was lined floor to ceiling with glass shelves holding refrigerated blood samples.

"What do you mean, my blood?" Bruce asked.

Sterns stopped and looked back at him. "Bruce, this is all you. You didn't send me much to work with, so I had to concentrate it and make more. With a little more trial and error, there's no end to what we can do! This gamma technology has limitless applications." He led them through the lab, filled with thousands of samples of Bruce's blood, cloned using technology Bruce had never seen. "This is potentially Olympian!" Sterns crowed. "We'll unlock hundreds of cures. We will make humans impervious to disease!"

Pure horror darkened Bruce's face—this was his worst nightmare coming true! The Hulk in his blood was now loose in these test tubes. "No, no. We've got to destroy it," Bruce broke in.

"Wait, what—what —?" Dr. Sterns sputtered.

"All of it," Bruce insisted. "Tonight. We're going to incinerate it. Is this the whole supply?"

Dr. Sterns gulped, and his cheerful expression vanished. "But..." he whined. "We could get the Nobel Prize for this!"

Bruce shook his head firmly. "You don't understand the power of this thing. It is too dangerous. It cannot be controlled."

"But we've got the antidote now!" Dr. Sterns argued. "This is Promethean fire!"

From the rooftop nearby, the snipers watched Bruce move in front of the window. They raised their rifles in anticipation. Then Betty shifted in front of Bruce, blocking the clean shot.

"At your discretion, shooter," Sparr told the snipers. She was listening in to Dr. Sterns's raving and thought the best thing to do would be take them all out. But she had her orders.

"Almost..." one sniper reported over the radio. "No, no shot."

Downstairs, Blonsky lost his patience and bolted into a stairwell.

Sparr saw him on one of the other soldiers' cameras. She turned to General Ross. "Blonsky's going in!"

"Blonsky, stand down!" Ross ordered. "My daughter's in there!"

But Blonsky was jumping up the stairs with astounding leaps, running up eight flights in seconds. He jumped up whole floors from railing to railing, moving so fast Sparr had a hard time tracking his progress.

Back in the lab, Sterns was trying to convince Bruce that everything was under control. "We have the antidote now!" Sterns protested.

"They don't want the antidote!" Bruce yelled at Dr. Sterns. "They want to make it a weapon. And if we let it go, we will never get it back. You don't have any idea how powerful this thing is."

Dr. Sterns waved his hands, dismissing Bruce's concerns. "Oh, I hate the government just as much as anyone," he said, "but you're being a little paranoid, don't you think?"

Bam! A hole appeared in the windowpane behind Bruce.

Bruce's eyes suddenly glazed over. He turned to reveal a tranquilizer dart sticking out the back of his neck.

Dr. Sterns screamed.

CHAPTER 21

Bruce's knees buckled, but Betty caught him before he fell. Then Blonsky burst through the lab door.

"No!" Betty screamed. She jumped in front of Bruce.

Blonsky smiled and shoved her aside—hard. Betty smashed into one of the lab cases. The glass shattered, and she cried out with pain.

Bruce's eyes flashed with anger, but they dimmed as he struggled to focus.

With a crazy laugh, Blonsky grabbed the front

of Bruce's shirt and shook him. Blonsky glared into Bruce's hazy eyes. "Come on!" he shouted. "Where is it?" He smacked Bruce across the face.

When he didn't get a reaction, Blonsky smacked him again.

Three more soldiers burst into the lab. "Blonsky!" one commando shouted.

"Show it to me!" Blonsky screamed at Bruce, and slapped him one more time. When Bruce didn't move, Blonsky backhanded him in the head, knocking him out cold.

The alley behind the lab was closed off by police vehicles. The command van backed up to the sidewalk outside the lab, its doors open. Sparr and Ross watched as Bruce, bound by enormous wrist shackles, was rolled out of the building on a gurney. There was a thick cold pack on his head where Blonsky hit him, and amazingly he was awake but groggy. Two soldiers escorted the gurney into the back of the van.

Betty had walked out of the building with the gurney, her wrist in a splint. Lingering to consult with a military medic behind her, she let Bruce go ahead of her.

As the gurney reached Ross, he stopped it and looked down into Bruce's dizzy eyes. Ross whispered, "If you took it from me, I'll put you in a hole for the rest of your life."

When Betty saw her father talking to Bruce, she hurried over, and Ross quickly waved the gurney into the van.

"Betty—" Ross began.

She turned around and said, "I will never forgive what you've done to him."

"He's a fugitive," Ross said.

"You made him a fugitive to cover your failures and protect your career," Betty said, her voice low and angry. "Don't ever speak to me as your daughter again."

"It's only because you're my daughter that you're not in handcuffs, too," Ross said, hiding his feelings as best he could.

Betty turned her back on him strode after the

gurney, climbing up into the ambulance. Ross just watched her go.

Sparr was upstairs in the lab questioning Dr. Sterns. "Are you telling me you can make more like him?"

"No, not yet." Sterns dabbed at the bridge of his nose, which had been cut by flying glass. "I sorted out a few pieces, but it's not like I can put together the same Humpty Dumpty, if that's what you're asking. He was a freak accident! The goal is to do it better!"

Sparr nodded. "So Banner's the only one we've got to worry about—"

She jerked suddenly, her eyes rolling. Then she slumped to the floor.

Blonsky was standing behind her. He'd just slammed her with the handle of his knife.

"Why are you always hitting people?" Dr. Sterns gasped.

Click! Blonsky pulled out a nasty-looking pistol, cocking it in Dr. Sterns's face.

"Now what could I have possibly done to deserve such aggression?" Sterns said, trying to sound defiant.

"It's not what you've done. It's what you're going to

do," Blonsky said. "I want what you got out of Banner. I want that."

Dr. Sterns peered at Blonsky. His face changed, and he stood up, suddenly unafraid of the gun. "You've got something extra in you already, don't you?"

"I want more," Blonsky said. "You've seen what he becomes, right?"

"I have," Dr. Sterns replied. "It's beautiful. Godlike."

"Well, I want that. I need that. Make me that," Blonsky said. His face was contorted, like there was something inside of him that he didn't know how to let out.

Dr. Sterns raised his eyebrows. "I don't know what you've got inside you already. The mix could be...an abomination."

Blonsky grabbed Dr. Sterns by the front of his shirt and lifted him straight up in the air with one arm. His other hand still held the gun.

"I didn't say I was unwilling," Dr. Sterns gasped. "I just need informed consent."

Blonsky lowered him.

"And you've given it," Dr. Sterns said.

Minutes later, Blonsky was lying on the lab table, and Dr. Sterns had hooked him up to the cell-saturation machine. The professor rapidly attached a "Mr. Green" blood canister to the infusion port, and then slid the gamma machine's emitter into place.

Blonsky looked up at his reflection in the silver disk of the emitter and saw white crosshairs moving over his forehead.

When the procedure began, everything started to go wrong right away. The surge of energy from Blonsky's body sent all the lab machinery into a frenzy of short circuits and blinking lights. The power went out in part of the lab. "This is what I was trying to explain!" Sterns cried out over the noise. "I don't know what you've been ladling into yourself."

He turned around and was stunned at what he saw. Blonsky was no longer on the table, and...something...was moving in the darkened part of the lab. Sterns could see enough to tell that it was no ordinary human. He could hear the difference, too. This thing growled like he imagined a dragon, or some other mythological beast, might.

"But clearly it worked," he said, and swallowed. His throat was suddenly dry. "Let's assume you don't understand a word I'm saying...but if you'll just get back on the table, I can fix this."

The monster that had been Emil Blonsky stepped out of the shadows. It laughed, a sound like rocks grinding together, and swatted Dr. Sterns aside. As it left the lab, there were sounds of gunfire from the soldiers standing guard.

Sterns lay where he had fallen, his eyes glazed from the blow he had taken. Some of the Banner blood dripped onto his head from the cracked canister...and as he lay there, Dr. Samuel Sterns began to change as well.

The helicopter buzzed through the night sky over the Hudson River. Ross sat up front with his intelligence team while Bruce and Betty sat on benches across from each other in the rear, both flanked by soldiers. Betty tapped Bruce's foot with her own, trying to reassure him without drawing anyone's attention.

The radio crackled.

"Delta Four to leader!" cried a panicky voice. "They took out two of our guys, repeat two of our guys! Blonsky and the major are still inside!" On the radio, they could all hear the sounds of explosions and chaos.

The radio squawked with an enormous crash and a bone-chilling roar of rage.

"The Hulk is in the street! Repeat, the Hulk is in the street!" the soldier cried into the radio.

Ross glanced down the helicopter interior at Bruce, who stared back at him.

"That's impossible," Ross said into the radio. "You get hold of yourself, young man. You get it together. What is your position?"

"One hundred twenty-first Street, headed north on Broadway!" the soldier shouted.

"Turn us around," Ross ordered.

The helicopter banked sharply.

"We're going back," Bruce said. "Why are we going back?"

"Give me eyes down there!" Ross barked.

"Yes, sir!" On Ross's screen appeared the feed from one of the soldiers' cameras. It showed a giant figure rampaging through the streets. Like the Hulk...only bigger. Much bigger.

CHAPTER 22

The helicopter swooped toward Harlem, where explosions and commotion could already be seen from the air.

Ross stared at the video monitors as the soldier raced up a street parallel to the creature who was wreaking havoc. He caught a glimpse of the monster's rear flank, with smashed cars rolling in its wake, but then it disappeared behind a building. It had looked Hulk-like, but the view had been too brief.

"I said get me eyes on that thing!" Ross shouted.

Bruce pushed past the soldier guarding him and joined Ross by the monitors. Betty quickly followed.

On the monitor, the vehicle had reached 125th Street. It slammed on the brakes, and the video picture lurched around. When the image settled, Ross's, Bruce's, and Betty's jaws dropped. They could see a massive, brownish-green creature gleefully causing chaos. Pedestrians fled in panic, and cars skidded, smashing into hydrants.

"Sir, are you seeing this?" the soldier called. "Is that Banner?" he continued, his voice trembling.

"It's not Banner!" Ross snapped. "Hold position!"

The monster stomped toward the vehicle, and the occupants of the helicopter got their first good look. The creature was at least fourteen feet tall and ridiculously muscled. He was as brawny as the Hulk, but he had strange bone spurs protruding along his ankles and wrists and down his spine.

The camera panned up to his snarling face—a face they all instantly recognized.

"One of yours?" Bruce asked. He knew the answer,

but he wanted to hear Thunderbolt Ross say it out loud.

"Oh my God," Betty said. "What have you done?"

On the streets, police and soldiers were hitting this new Abomination with everything they had. But nothing worked. The two soldiers in the vehicle unloaded on it with a rocket-propelled grenade. It didn't even flinch...but they did get Blonsky's attention. He charged down the street after the automobile, which slammed into reverse and roared away back south.

"Get out of there, soldier!" Ross commanded.

But the Abomination was too fast. It ran close to the vehicle, which was caroming off parked cars as it fled in reverse. The Abomination picked up a taxicab and held it overhead. Huge fireballs backlit the creature, showing off its spines and the bones interlaced with its huge muscles. The soldier's camera tracked it all.

The Abomination loomed over the camera. He leered down, holding the taxicab high.

"Give me a real fight!" he roared. Then he brought the taxi down.

The camera fuzzed out, and the monitor went black.

Ross, Bruce, and Betty sat in silence.

Then the radio squawked again. "General," a communications officer said, "the NYPD want to know what to use against it. What do you want me to tell them? Sir?"

Ross stared silently at the dead monitor.

"Sir?" the communications officer prompted again over the radio.

Ross shook off his shock. "Tell them to bring everything they've got and head for Harlem," he ordered. He lowered his head. "And heaven help them," he whispered. The general's face was tired and grim— he knew the military had no way to fight the monster.

"It has to be me," Bruce said, knowing there was no other choice. "You have to take me back there."

"What are you saying?" Betty asked him. "You think you can control it?"

"No, not control it, but...I don't know. Maybe aim it."

"And what if you can't?" Ross snapped.

"We made this thing. All of us," Bruce said. "Please."

Ross closed his eyes, then slowly nodded his head. "Land us near it," he instructed the pilot.

"No, no. Keep us high," Bruce interrupted. "Open the back door."

Ross nodded. A soldier hit a button, and the ramp of the helicopter hinged open. Cool air rushed inside.

Bruce hurried toward the rear, still locked in the wrist shackles. "Put me over it!" He instructed. "Go higher!"

The helicopter surged upward, and the city dropped away. Bruce peered down from the open door. New York was three thousand feet below them, glowing in the darkness. Another explosion boomed up in Harlem, but from that height, Bruce couldn't hear the screams.

"Bruce, stop! What are you doing?" Betty yelled. "Think about this. You don't even know if you'll change." She had hold of his arm. "You don't have to do this. Please, this is insane!"

"Betty, I've got to try," Bruce said. "I'm sorry."

He kissed her, letting his lips linger on hers...and then he let go, falling back out of the open cargo door.

The wind whooshed around him as he tumbled down toward 125th street. He closed his eyes and let himself fall.

He fell. And fell.

Nothing happened. No burst of energy or anger or power.

Nothing.

Bruce's eyes snapped open. Uh-oh, he thought.

He plunged at unbelievable speed toward the street below.

CHAPTER 23

Bruce Banner crashed into the Harlem street in an explosion of asphalt and dirt, leaving a very deep, rough hole in the pavement.

Down the street, the Abomination was inflicting terrible destruction on the city, and civilians running from his path dodged the hole in the ground from all directions.

A mighty green hand and arm rose up and grabbed

the hole's ragged edge, crushing the street with its grip. The Hulk emerged from the ground.

All around were police lights flashing, people running, sirens blaring, and explosions detonating in the distance. A police chopper aimed its spotlight on the Abomination down the street. The Hulk staggered, unable to stand the sensory overload of a city in chaos.

But then the Hulk closed his eyes, grimacing against the madness. He strained, all his muscles flexing, and he let out a roar, shaking his head to clear it.

Now he could concentrate on his target: the Abomination—the enemy.

The Hulk stood tall and bellowed at his adversary, his roar shaking the street.

The Abomination turned around and saw the Hulk. His gray eyes shimmered with malicious recognition. "Hulk," he growled.

Hurtling toward each other, the two giants collided so powerfully that the windows of the surrounding storefronts shattered. A theater's marquee exploded into a fountain of sparks. The Abomination tackled the Hulk, knocking him off his feet, and they tumbled down the street toward Broadway, ripping up the asphalt as they rolled. The Abomination got his feet first and flung Hulk away. The force of the impact on the ground staggered the Hulk, who took a moment to recover his senses. Just then, the Abomination approached, striding through the fires blazing in the wrecked cars that littered the street.

"Come on," the Abomination said, beckoning.

The Hulk turned to a police car abandoned nearby. Its wailing siren irritated him. He smashed it down flat and then tore it in half, holding the two halves, as he had held the pieces of the sculpture the last time he'd faced Blonsky. He charged at the Abomination and began to beat him with the pieces of the car. The Abomination lost his balance and landed on his back. The Hulk pounded him with the car until it came apart, then pounded him with his fists. The pavement was cracked and caved in all around them.

The Abomination turned his head and spat. Then he said, "Is that all you've got?"

The Hulk reared back to deliver another punch, and the Abomination got his revenge for the fight in the field. He kicked the Hulk so hard that Hulk's flying body punched straight through the nearest building.

The Abomination rumbled down the street, accelerated like a long jumper, and soared up into the side of the first building, digging massive handholds into the bricks as he scaled the apartment. When he got to the hole left by the Hulk's body, he could see to the street on the other side.

Above them, the helicopter buzzed low over Harlem. General Ross and Betty watched the battle from the copter. Betty gasped as she saw the Hulk crash through the building and come down behind it, pulverizing a large waste container when he landed.

General Ross peered down from the helicopter over the gunner's narrow shoulder, narrowing his eyes as he saw the Abomination climbing. "Use that weapon, soldier!" Ross ordered the gunner. "Give him some help!"

"Which one?" the gunner asked.

"Shoot that one climbing the wall!" Ross retorted. "Which one do you think?"

Tracer fire streaked down in the dark as the gunner blasted the helicopter's cannon down at the Abomination. Bricks exploded around the climbing creature.

The Abomination managed to reach the rooftop, where the gunner had a clearer shot. Cannon rounds streaked down at him, ripping up the roof. Some of the rounds ricocheted off the Abomination's plate-like bones, but others stung him enough to slow him down...a little.

The Abomination headed for a water tower, sprinting across the roof with the helicopter tight overhead. Betty clung to the helicopter's ramp as it accelerated to keep up.

Down in the alley, the Hulk heard the sound of firing above. He shook himself, growled, and then bounced off the close walls of the alley, scaling the space parkour-style.

When he reached the top, he jumped onto the remaining fire escape and pulled himself onto the roof.

The helicopter hovered to his left, raining cannon

fire down on the Abomination's back. The Abomination changed course, sprinting toward the helicopter as the Hulk got to the rooftop. The Abomination ran to the edge of the building and jumped. Up on the ramp, Betty's eyes widened in fear. If the Abomination hit the chopper, it would never survive the impact.

The Hulk sprinted across the roof toward the Abomination and and lunged just as the creature jumped. He caught the Abomination's legs, dragging him down so that all the beast could do was catch hold of one of the helicopter's landing skids. The machine lurched and spun around as the pilot tried to keep control with an extra two tons of the Hulk and the Abomination struggling below.

"I can't hold it!" the pilot shouted. "I've got to put it down!"

Betty lurched across the rear ramp, barely managing to hang on. They had gotten close to the Grayburn College campus again. The helicopter spun and pitched in the air. Below it, the Hulk and the Abomination collided with rooftop cisterns and the corners of buildings.

The helicopter was going to crash. The rear rotor had failed, and it was a miracle it hadn't gone down in flames already. Inside the copter, Ross hung on to his chair, his jaw set firmly.

Betty closed her eyes.

CHAPTER 24

The helicopter spun wildly around its main rotor, narrowly clearing the top of the college's library. It skittered into the dome of the main hall and crashed down into the plaza. Betty was hurled toward the front of the cabin as the tail rotor sheared off, and the rear ramp crumpled like a crushed can. The Abomination was under the copter when it hit the ground. Its rotors shattered against his back. The Hulk had tumbled free.

Inside, Betty recovered her senses first. She saw her father wedged up against the pilot's chair. "Dad? Are you hurt? Let me help you."

"I'm all right," General Ross groaned. "Just find a way out."

The crashed helicopter shook as the Abomination climbed on top of it, finding the Hulk in the main plaza of Grayburn College. The Abomination leaped off the copter and slammed the Hulk against a marble wall, pounding his body like a boxer against the ropes. The Hulk clinched him to stop the pummeling, their faces inches apart, teeth bared with strain.

He struggled against the Abomination's grip but could not get free. Behind the creature, Hulk saw Betty trying to get out of the crashed helicopter.

The Abomination guessed where he was looking, and his grin got even wider. "You don't deserve this power," the Abomination said with a leer. "Now watch her die."

The Abomination raised his gigantic right forearm and pinned it against the Hulk's throat, the elbow spike driving into the flesh of the Hulk's chest, right above his thumping heart. The marble wall cracked behind the Hulk's head.

Blood poured down the Hulk's chest, but he found a reserve of strength in his desperation to save Betty. Fire was spreading in the wrecked helicopter, and its fuel tanks were leaking on the plaza. Soon it would explode!

The Hulk caught both of the Abomination's wrists in his hands and forced them apart, roaring with the exertion. He drove his knee up into the beast's belly, twice, knocking the breath out of him. Then he pivoted and drove the Abomination headfirst into the wall. The Abomination was stunned for a moment, and the Hulk leaped clear...just as the first spark hit the spreading pool of helicopter fuel with a blinding whoosh of flame.

Halfway there, the Hulk saw that he wouldn't be able to beat the explosion. Still running, he slammed his hands together in a thunderous clap. The shock wave blew the fire out and rocked everyone inside. But their lives were saved. They staggered to their feet.

Betty gasped as she heard a crackling, rattling sound from behind the Hulk and saw the Abomination had gotten up again. "Look out!" she cried.

The Hulk turned but not in time. A tremendous blow to the side of his head bowled him over. He tried to rise, dazed, staring up at the Abomination looming above him.

The Abomination had fashioned a weapon out of a chain with two huge steel weights at one end. He swung it over his head like a nunchaku, and the weights smashed the Hulk to the side again. He lay sprawled, trying to get his feet under him again, but the blow would have knocked the library building down. The Hulk couldn't just shake it off.

Now the Abomination advanced on the helicopter, again whirling the huge steel weights over his head. "General," he said, gloating, "any last words?"

He raised his arms, ready to bring the weights down and crush the helicopter to fragments...with Betty, General Ross, and the rest of the crew in it.

General Ross didn't offer any words. But the Hulk did.

The Hulk struggled to his knees, then pulled his feet under himself in a squat and roared, "Hulk...smash!"

As the Abomination swung his weapon, the Hulk smashed his enormous fists into the ground to throw his enemy off balance. The force of the Hulk's fists formed a canyon in the ground.

The Abomination stumbled and slipped straight through the crack in the ground. As he fell, the chain from his weapon swung free through the air, circling the Abomination's enormous neck. The Hulk didn't hesitate. He launched himself on the Abomination and yanked the chain tightly. He dragged the Abomination back with all his strength as the Abomination fought, lashing his fists and elbows backward to pound the Hulk's head and shoulders. But the Hulk was too angry to care. He was going to end this now. The Abomination would never hurt anyone, or threaten anyone, again.

But Betty had gotten out of the helicopter, and now she stood in front of the Hulk and screamed out, "Stop!"

The Abomination hung limp in Hulk's grip...but he was not dead yet. The Hulk paused and looked at Betty...then, incredibly, he let the overcome Abomination drop to the ground. Around them, soldiers and police officers lowered their weapons.

The Hulk and Betty walked to each other amid the wreckage. Betty looked up at him. "It's okay," she said.

The Hulk reached out and stroked her cheek, wiping away a tear from when she had been so scared that he would die. He looked at it, then looked back at her. Slowly, working hard for each syllable, he said, "Betty."

A helicopter spotlight pinned him, and he flinched. Then, with a last look at Betty, he turned and ran, bounding across the rooftops to escape. Betty watched him go. Then she turned to General Ross. He was watching her, and Betty knew he had seen the truth.

The Hulk had turned into a hero.

EPILOGUE

etty Ross stood at the railing looking south over New York Harbor from Battery Park City. She was thinking of the last time she had come this way, on the boat with Bruce from New Jersey. She wondered what had ever happened to that pickup they'd driven up from Tennessee and then abandoned at the mouth of the Holland Tunnel.

And she wondered what had happened to Bruce.

She still had the picture of him on her camera,

from right before they got into the truck. She kept it. She would always keep it...and the next time she saw Bruce, she would take another one. He would come back when he was ready, when he could really control the Hulk. Betty knew. She would wait.

In a cabin in the wilderness of western Canada, Bruce got his mail. There was a small package addressed to David B., which was the name Bruce had used in a certain business transaction. He opened the package and removed the necklace Betty had pawned for traveling money. He'd looked for quite a while before tracking it down, but now he had it.

Bruce sealed it in an envelope, addressed it to Betty, and put a stamp on the envelope. He would mail it in the morning, and when Betty got it, she would know he was thinking of her.

Then Bruce meditated. Every day he got a little better at keeping the beast inside. But he wouldn't be able to hold it in forever. That wouldn't matter as long

as he could control it...and where he had once meditated to hold the monster in, now Bruce was learning
how to use meditation to bring the change into the
Hulk when he wanted it. On his terms.

He practiced. He kept practicing.

One of these days, when he had it right, he would
find Betty again.

Just off-base in Florida, Thunderbolt Ross finished
his drink.

He was not feeling good. The Super-Soldier project
was a disaster and so was General Thunderbolt Ross's
career. The Abomination had destroyed everything
Ross had worked for, and to make matters worse,
Bruce Banner was the one who had saved New
York—and Betty—from the monster Emil Blonsky
had become.

The bartender came back and poured him another
one. Ross could see himself in the mirror and didn't
like what he saw. What was next? He'd have to retire.

He'd put his feet up, go fishing, and have to chew on his failures for the rest of his life.

And Betty still wouldn't talk to him. He had people watching her, and she hadn't been in touch with Bruce, either. No one seemed to know where Bruce was. At moments like this, that suited Ross fine. Bruce Banner could fall right off the face of the Earth, and it wouldn't bother Ross a bit.

Someone else came in and walked up next to him. "Mmmm, the smell of defeat," he said. "You know, I hate to say 'I told you so,' General, but that Super-Soldier program was put on ice for a reason." Ross knew without looking up that it was Tony Stark speaking to him. Stark, better known as Iron Man, was everything Thunderbolt Ross was not. He was rich, he was popular, he was a big shot inside S.H.I.E.L.D., and his Iron Man project—unlike Ross's Super-Soldier project—was a roaring success.

"I've always felt hardware was much more reliable," Stark said.

General Ross turned a weary glare on Stark's photogenic face. "Stark."

Stark nodded. "General."

Thunderbolt Ross didn't like Tony Stark, and both of them knew it. But occasionally they had been forced to work together.

"You always wear such nice suits," Ross said, mocking Tony's reliance on armored suits instead of his own strength.

Tony looked down at himself. He was in fact wearing a nice suit. It had cost a lot of money. "Touché," he said. "I hear you have an unusual problem."

"You should talk," Ross said. He knew some of what had been going on at Stark Industries lately.

"You should listen," Stark said, getting more serious. "What if I told you we were putting a team together?"

"Who's 'we'?" Ross asked.

That's when Tony Stark sat down and started talking.

TURN THE PAGE FOR AN
EXCITING PREVIEW OF

MARVEL CINEMATIC UNIVERSE
PHASE ONE

MARVEL

T H O R

The All-Father did not act without thought. Now, as the sun shone over Asgard and the buildings were illuminated by its rays, gleaming like gold, he thought long and hard. At the realm's edge, the darkness of the cosmos spread out like a calm sea. Asgard was at peace, and all was ready for the momentous events to come.

Standing in his chambers, Odin stared out at the realm he had ruled for so many years. Despite the beauty before him, his mind was troubled and his expression drawn with worry and tension.

As All-Father, Odin had battled great beasts, invaded foreign realms, destroyed strong enemies, and kept the realm of Asgard safe and peaceful. He had lost his brothers and father to war. For thousands upon thousands of years, he had carried the burden of his crown alone. It had wearied him at times, energized him at others. When he had married his wife, Frigga, the burden had lifted, as she was a strong partner and had a helpful ear. And with the birth of his first son, Thor, Odin had felt hopeful that one day he would be able to pass along his crown to a worthy successor and find the peace he so rightly deserved.

Now that day had finally come. For today, Thor would become king.

Yet Odin did not feel a sense of relief.

With a deep sigh, he turned from the wide doorway that led out to his chamber balcony. Behind him, the two giant statues of his fallen brothers standing outside the palace framed his tired body, dwarfing him, while at the same time hinting at his great might and heritage. He was not yet dressed for the evening, still in the golden robes that he would soon exchange for his ceremonial gear. But his hair was combed and his face freshly shaved. Odin's shoulder-length hair was no longer the rich brown of his youth, but the gray suited him and he still had the bearing of a great warrior and powerful leader.

Queen Frigga sat at her vanity, putting on her jewelry. In the reflection, she saw her husband turn and come back into the center of the room. His blue eyes were dark with worry, and she felt a now long-familiar rush of love. She had married a warrior, but knew him as so much more than that. He did not rule lightly. Everything he had done and everything he would do was the result of great reflection. He had seen the results of battles that had not been thought out and had lost too many warriors to unnecessary violence. And so she knew that he had thought long and hard about this day.

While some argued that Thor should have assumed the throne years ago, Odin had seen the benefit in waiting. He wanted his son to follow in his footsteps and the footsteps of his father before him—to keep Asgard safe and free of war. Yet Thor was not his father. Thor was impulsive and hotheaded. He still had much to learn about the value of patience. Alas, Odin had no more time left to teach. He was growing weaker by the day. Soon, he would need to enter the Odinsleep, during which he would be unable to rule, his body in a state of suspended animation while he used the powerful Odinforce to rejuvenate.

Feeling his wife's gaze on him, Odin looked up and smiled, the corners of his eyes crinkling. She continued to amaze him. Her beauty was beyond compare, and while servants rushed about in preparation below, she sat calmly, her back straight and her head high. Now, more than ever, he needed her strength.

"Do you think he's ready?" Odin asked, his voice deep with emotion.

She looked at him and nodded slowly. "Thor has his father's wisdom," she said, knowing that was what he needed to hear. But Odin's expression remained worried, so she added, "He won't be alone. Loki will be at his side to give him counsel."

She stood up and approached her husband. Loki,

their younger son, was a source of tension between them. Odin had always favored Thor because Thor was a warrior, just like him, but Loki was not, and so his younger had formed a closer bond with Queen Frigga. But in a way, that had been a good balance. Loki was Thor's opposite—quiet, thoughtful, and content to stay in the shadows. Frigga hoped that Odin would see the benefit of having the brothers side by side.

He reached out a hand, about to caress her cheek. But he stopped suddenly.

Odin's hand was shaking. The All-Father stood staring at it with fierce concentration, as though willing it to stop. "If only we had more time," Odin said when his hand finally stopped shaking. "I can fight it a little longer...."

Frigga held up a hand. "No! You've put it off too long!" she said harshly. Then her expression softened. "I worry for you."

Odin cocked his head, a playful smile tugging at his lips. "I've destroyed demons and monsters, devastated whole worlds, laid waste to mighty kingdoms, and still you worry for me?"

"Always," Frigga answered truthfully. She knew what he was capable of, but she still feared that Thor's new role would be Odin's undoing.

But she didn't have to worry. Her words had reassured her husband as they always did, and now, for better or worse, he was ready to pass the throne on to his elder son.

In a few short minutes, the mighty Thor would succeed his father and become the new king of Asgard. All attention would be on him, just as he liked it. No one would notice Thor's younger brother. No one would notice Loki the Trickster. And that's just the way Loki liked it.